COMMUNITY HOSPITAL

COMMUNITY HOSPITAL

AS SEEN BY A WOMAN DOCTOR

Angela Sréter Spencer

COMMUNITY HOSPITAL
AS SEEN BY A WOMAN DOCTOR

iUniverse books may be ordered through booksellers or by contacting:

iUniverse
1663 Liberty Drive
Bloomington, IN 47403
www.iuniverse.com
844-349-9409

ISBN: 978-1-6632-1018-0 (sc)
ISBN: 978-1-6632-1019-7 (e)

Library of Congress Control Number: 2020925088

Print information available on the last page.

iUniverse rev. date: 12/21/2020

CONTENTS

Dedication vii
Acknowledgments...ix
Outline xi

Chapter 1... 1
Chapter 2... 9
Chapter 3... 15
Chapter 4... 20
Chapter 5... 26
Chapter 6... 34
Chapter 7... 41
Chapter 8... 47
Chapter 9... 54
Chapter 10... 67
Chapter 11... 74
Chapter 12... 83
Chapter 13... 89
Chapter 14... 96
Chapter 15... 105
Chapter 16... 113
Chapter 17... 120
Chapter 18... 126
Chapter 19... 138

Chapter 20...142
Chapter 21...155
Chapter 22...160
Chapter 23...166
Chapter 24...175
Chapter 25...181
Chapter 26...186
Chapter 27...193
Chapter 28...203
Chapter 29...209
Chapter 30...219
Chapter 31...226

About the Author 235

DEDICATION

Like sunshine and shadow, medicine is practiced by altruistic professionals and individuals who take it merely as a job. I dedicate this work to those, who with their knowledge, skills, and compassion make a lifelong commitment to help the ill.

ACKNOWLEDGMENTS

We all experience unexpected, life-changing events in our lives. To a large extent, our survival depends on the people who surround and help us. Without the assistance and dexterity of some, and the love and compassion of others, we may not have been here, to tell our story.

Hard-working professionals deserve my sincere and heartfelt thanks, because without them, I would not have made it. Strong women friends, like Sonna Whiteley, Debbie Frazier, Maggie Ostergard, Diana Steele, and many others, stood by me and assisted me without being asked. My family, especially my two loving sons, Tom Z. Fabian, Ph.D. and Gabor E. Fabian, confirmed my life was not in vain, and assured me that many parts of me would survive to the end and remain immortal.

My Editors-In-Chief, Susan Gauthier and Dale Steele corrected my punctuation errors and edited my text into a refined and more enjoyable read. The patients and colleagues who provided me with the material and the valuable suggestions of my friends are highly appreciated.

I extend my sincerest thanks to all.

OUTLINE

This exceedingly relevant and entertaining novel sheds light on our contemporary health care setting and its providers. All stories are true, only the names and places are changed to protect the innocent and guilty alike. This book is written with the hope to assist the general public in challenging situations, when they need it the most. It also aims to bear testimony to the many unsung heroes who have sacrificed everything for their profession.

Contemporary health care, with tremendous demands being made on it, is changing rapidly. Medicine has seen many conventional, empathic, and knowledgeable practitioners, but recently, a large number of result-driven, business-oriented people have made their way to this profession. An otherwise honest mistake made by the latter is often wrapped in arrogance. Their inability to manage time properly may result in oversight, hasty, and erroneous judgments, or outright, deliberate falsification, to the detriment of their patients.

Much medical ineptness is buried with the extremely tolerant patients. Although faults may be recognized by one or more parties, blunders are not openly discussed. Silence causes them to quietly and relentlessly propagate and disseminate into a practice. Not many patients possess health related information, medical knowledge, and legal familiarity combined with personal stamina, indomitable will, and utmost tenacity to live the truth.

The reception of unpleasant news regarding one's own health will be unexpected and result in fear. The emotional turmoil when receiving such news is further aggravated by information that is incomplete or ambiguous; information that is offered in largely incomprehensible medical specific terminology. It is important to have another person present at every encounter with a professional, whether it is in healthcare or in legal matters. The old saying of "Two people are better than one" never had been more valid than by having an extra set of eyes and ears. Detailed inquiry, cautious acceptance, and respectful discussion are of paramount importance.

Considerate co-operation could be key to a successful doctor-patient relationship. Until such a relationship has been established, all patients need a reliable and educated advocate who can assist them at all times. This patient advocate can also help them navigate through the dangerous and often uncharted areas of medical diagnosis and treatment. (See the hospital's Health Care Surrogate if you don't understand what the doctor is saying.)

1

What does love look like? It has the hands to help others.
It has the feet to hasten to the poor and needy. It has
eyes to see misery and want. It has the ears to hear the
sighs and sorrows of men. That is what love looks like.

―――――――

Saint Augustine

"When I was sixteen, I knew the answer to everything. I am sixty today and I have realized, how little did I know. I certainly have answers only to a few things." Marsha S. Redcliff, MD calmly answered as she smiled at the Chairman of the Credentialing Committee.

Earlier, at the introductions, she noted that the six members who comprised the group were all physicians in various medical specialties. A nephrologist, a surgeon, two internists, an endocrinologist, and a hospitalist were sitting around a large, round conference table. The chairman was a good looking pulmonologist in his early fifties. These seven men were to decide whether or not Dr. Redcliff was a needed and desired addition to the practicing physicians of Cecilia Beach Community Hospital. Each of the men felt that there was very little need to further question the applicant, because some had known her work from the previous years when she had completed her fellowship here, and the others were simply impressed by her resume. All felt this investigation was a formality only, yet to maintain the importance of their function, they were obligated to continue the inquiries. It was no secret that the hospital badly needed a neurologist and there was no one else to apply for the position, anyway.

"I see, you have developed a healthy insight. I can't help but wonder how your philosophy of life affects your patient care. I hope you don't project too often the uncertainty to answer them." The surgeon's rapidly fired words stung Marsha. The others curiously waited for her response.

"You can be assured; I know my area of medicine. I know what to do and how to handle a neurology case. I am sure you do the very same in the area of your expertise. I have never been sued, and as a matter of fact, never been named in a malpractice suit. My patients stay with me for a long time. This alone should answer you." Marsha talked directly to the man but her firm tone was duly noted by all.

"I referred only to the fact that learning is an incessant process and that we all learn throughout our lives." She looked at each man at the table before she continued in an even tone. "The more information and experience we gather, the more we should realize that we can grasp only a small part of the world's extensive knowledge. Wisdom is the combination of learning and understanding our limitations. Years ago, while in Europe, I stumbled upon a profoundly true poem. In rough translation, it described the wheat plant which proudly raises its head toward the sky while it's green, but unassumingly lowers itself to the earth when ripe. It is the same with people: the schoolchild brags with his treasure of knowledge, while a sagacious man humbles himself. Don't you find it astonishingly beautiful?"

"It is. Thank you for sharing it with us. It's clear to me that you want to help people. You must like them; otherwise you can't say these things. Can you?" The endocrinologist chimed in.

"Yes, I do. I respect people. My motto is *'Do unto others as you would have them do unto you.'* I was given two hands, and one is enough for my own help. The other I must use to help everyone else. I am paraphrasing the late Audrey Hepburn's saying."

"My, you must have retained some of the wide-eyed, childhood optimism we all had in medical school. Of course, you recently graduated, didn't you? Unfortunately, the enthusiasm quickly erodes once you encounter the public. We all had patients who did a good job on turning the sunny outlook to a more realistic, stark, and entirely scientific approach." Evidently, the surgeon just couldn't let his opinion be unknown.

"My graduation date has nothing to do with my optimism. Indeed, I was the oldest in my class to graduate, and by far the oldest in my residency to finish the four years. In spite of my age, I graduated Cum Laude, and was elected Resident of the Year. Afterward, I wasn't resting on my laurels and added a year of fellowship to learn more about cerebrovascular diseases. I was told to be the oldest fresh neurologist ever to take the board examination; not quite a dinosaur, but probably close to it. And do you know what? I didn't mind it, because I have never regretted my decision to become a doctor. From my early childhood, that's all I ever wanted to be. Then life took some unexpected turns, and only after my sons completed their education, I got the chance to act upon my dream. It wasn't easy, but I did it." Marsha no longer cared what the seven people thought of her. This was her life, these were her accomplishments, and

3

she did not need to glorify anything in order to impress anyone.

"So you were a late-bloomer." The chairman quickly interjected to defuse the escalating mood. "There is nothing wrong with that. Actually, it is rather remarkable, don't you think that?"

"You said you always wanted to become a physician. Why? There must have been some reason that inspired you so deeply, that throughout life, it kept your dream alive. What was that?" The endocrinologist seemed genuinely interested.

"I came from a close-knit family. At every holiday, we all gathered at the home of my grandparents. I was particularly close to them. My grandmother was a remarkable woman. In addition to her nine children, she also raised four orphans. She never had a moment for her own wishes, never smoked, never drank; she only worked her hands to the bones. Then she got diagnosed with pancreatic cancer. I watched her go downhill. She endured a horrible pain, especially towards the end. During the ten months of her illness, she got one shot of pain medication. One. A single injection, that gave her relief for maybe four hours. One single pain shot, because the doctor said he did not want her to get addicted to morphine. Even as a child, I thought, it wouldn't have mattered if she got addicted for a month or two. At least she did not have to suffer. But no, the doctor disregarded my childish ideas and was adamant. That's when I decided if I ever became a doctor, I would never do that. That's when I also became determined that all patients needed someone to stand up and talk for them. I think that's why I became a physician."

"Whoa, that's powerful." The endocrinologist seemed to express everyone's opinion.

After a long pause, the surgeon broke the silence.

"You will never recoup your investments, I hope you realize. Medicine is not what it used to be, for sure." Most seemed to agree with him.

"I am well aware of that. Many people told me the same, believe me. I didn't become a physician for the money. If money were my only motivation, I would have entered politics. If I did not want to work with people, I should have chosen to work with computers or brick and mortar. Of course, I need money, but only to support myself, to make a living, and not to buy a mansion or a yacht. No one can eat with two spoons or wear more than one dress."

"That's refreshing to hear," the hospitalist smiled at Marsha, "I hope you never get disappointed. I think you would fit right in."

"I wanted to be effective, to help by curing an illness, to make a change by improving life. I was so convinced of my destiny that I sold my house and gave all my inheritance to my medical school."

"This restores my faith in people, I tell you," the endocrinologist smiled at Marsha, "I hope you never get disappointed. I think you would fit right in, you would get along with everyone nicely."

"I am sure the physicians would like you alright. The nursing staff might be another story." The hospitalist interjected, evidently speaking of his own experience.

"I never had problems with any of the nurses. I had been an RN before I went to medical school. I am familiar with their work and respect them. It's really interesting, but no matter what my position is, nurses always consider me as one of them. At least they can read my handwriting." Marsha laughed.

"Yes, but we have a wide spectrum of employees here. Some are from the Philippines, a few from Nigeria, and quite a few are American blacks. Would you respect them the same?" Marsha looked at the internist who clearly expected an answer but already seemed to doubt it. He had a wrinkled, gray turban, and a sparse beard, which most likely never had seen a barber.

"You hire only licensed nurses, don't you? They are educated, trained, and licensed. They know what they are doing. Just like the doctors who come from various backgrounds. Don't you agree?" The man remained quiet.

The chairman turned to Marsha. "In your job, you would have to educate the staff about the neurology disease symptoms, how to recognize them, and particularly raise awareness of stroke. The stroke coordinator is a black nurse. This is why we had to know your opinion."

"I work with people, doctors, and nurses. I don't work with white or black people. No one should." The room became still.

As if in a stage act, the door opened on cue. Quite unexpectedly, the CEO appeared with a pleasant smile and cheerful greeting. His sudden entrance saved them from further discussing an uncomfortable topic. The uneasiness almost instantly evaporated.

"Good evening, everyone. I was just going home when I noticed the lights in the conference room. What is the big occasion? Don't you think you should be heading home, too?"

"Dr. Jamison, we are confirming the appointment of the new neurologist. Let me introduce you to Dr. Marsha Redcliff, our candidate. Dr. Redcliff, this is Dr. Jamison, the hospital's CEO."

After the introduction Dr. Jamison comfortably placed himself in an armchair next to the chairman. Everyone else secretly wished him to leave so they could wrap up business and end the long day. Not noticing the sudden quietness, he started a jovial chat with Marsha.

"I read your resume, it's very impressive. From being a nurse and a nurse practitioner, you became a physician assistant, and then a physician. Why did you take the long road? Why did you not directly attend a medical school? Above all, you chose the most complex area, the most difficult specialty, neurology. I think we have to get you here, no question about it."

"I had obligations. My children's education was my primary responsibility. Only after my second son graduated from a university I could think about my own aspirations. Before that time, I took courses here and there and slowly accumulated enough credit to get my Master's Degree. But a medical school could not be done by piece-meal. It was an intense four-year stretch, every day, morning to night. When I finally could attend, I jumped at the opportunity. Anyway, thanks for asking, but the school years are over, thank goodness. So, here I am. Ready, able, and capable. The only question is when do you want me to start?"

They all looked at each other. Marsha Redcliff's sudden assertiveness was totally unexpected. The surgeon whispered something to the chairman, but before he could respond, Dr. Jamison announced his decision. "I vote for hiring Dr. Redcliff. Anyone has any objections? If you have anything to say against my recommendation, say it now." He looked around to note that all were in complete agreement with him. He was sure nobody would dare to disagree with him.

"In that case, let me be the first to congratulate you, Dr. Redcliff. I believe we just confirmed you. Welcome aboard."

Eight years later Marsha Redcliff was the only stroke specialist in the hospital. She chaired the multidisciplinary stroke committee and became the director of the Memory Disorder Clinic. She always encouraged her patients not to come to any office visits without bringing another set of ears and eyes along. She advised them to have an advocate, because as she said "The Devil never sleeps", and who knows what they would miss in a stressful situation.

As predicted, she never had a problem with any of her colleagues. The stroke coordinator became one of her greatest admirers and friend.

2

Nothing is so good as it seems beforehand.

George Eliot

Idyllic evening peace is seldom achieved and lasts only until the shrill sound of a phone shatters it.

Ed reached for the receiver, going more by the sound than actually seeing it, as the room was dark, and only a streak of yellow light coming from the monitor fell across the floor. After he got comfortable in his old armchair, he did not feel like getting up to switch the light on. His wife settled down in the next room with her latest romance novel, but apparently fell asleep with her glasses on her face and the book resting on her chest. Neither the light nor the sudden noise of the phone ringing bothered her.

"Hello. Yes, this is Mr. Jamison. What can I do for you?"

The voice was unfamiliar to Ed. The man sounded young, but over the phone it was difficult to say anything about his age. Ed suspected he must have been in his early thirties. He seemed a bit hesitant at first, but as he talked, he appeared to be more relaxed. On the other hand, Ed, who was relaxed in the beginning, became speechless with the growing tension. Stunned was really a better expression for what he felt, although he was not capable of thinking straight at that point.

"What did you say? Can you repeat it?"

The man started all over by introducing himself once more.

"So you are Gregory Wells. OK. What did you say before?"

"Listen, Mr. Jamison. I think we might be related. Please don't hang up the phone. Let me tell you what I know."

Ed pressed the receiver to his ear and glanced at his wife who appeared sleeping in the other room. She still was motionless on the sofa. *Good, she probably did not wake up to the phone ringing,* he thought.

"Where on earth would you get this idea, Mr. Wells?" He wanted to sound strong and indignant, but barely recognized his own voice as it sounded breathless, almost pleading.

"Mr. Jamison, let me tell you from the beginning. About a year and a half ago I joined a genealogy website. I wanted to know my background. You see, I never knew my father. My mother was in and out of my life. Most of the time she was hospitalized for mental illness and substance abuse. I grew up with my grandmother in Pennsylvania.

"No one knew anything about my father. No one could tell me who he was, or where he could be found. When my mother was young, she supported her drug habit by going with any man who paid for her drinks or got her dope. When I asked her about my father, she could not recall any names or any person, and just mentioned some of the cities and bars she frequented. I was at a loss.

"I think I turned eight when I learned I was named after Gregory Peck; not because my mother ever got even close to him, but because she had a crush on him.

Grandma told me about how much my mother adored Gregory Peck. She saw every movie he ever made, sometimes more than once. It was no surprise that she chose Gregory for my name.

"When they played one of Gregory Peck's movies in the local Ritz, I went to see him, expecting some revelation. I don't know what I was thinking, but at the age of eight, one can dream a lot. I came out of the theater sorely disappointed. Although he was quite handsome, I saw no resemblance. He was tall, dark, suntanned, and strikingly good-looking. I was small, blonde, pale, and blue eyed. Certainly nothing like him. I did not pay attention to him any further. I figured, he had nothing to do with me. I wanted my real father to be alive somewhere, not dead like what my grandma had told.

"When I was quite young, I did not miss my father. Then I saw other kids in my school who sometimes were picked up by their father. I knew they also went to play ball, fishing, or for summer vacations with their dad. I stayed with my grandmother. I imagined my father took me to places, pretended to talk with him about my daily problems, my school work, future plans, and said good night to him every evening before going to sleep. I was sure he looked like me, just bigger and stronger. I never told anyone about my dreams. We never talked about him at home. Slowly I realized grandma never mentioned him; she could not. She never knew who he was.

"Don't misunderstand me, Mr. Jamison. I loved my grandma. I just missed my father. When I was twenty-four, my mother died in a hospital. It did not shake me up. I really did not spend any time with her, never really knew her. On the other hand, when grandma passed, that was completely different. I loved her. She was the only family I had. My saving grace was my wife, Sharon. We were expecting our first child and we named her after my grandma. Moriah is fifteen now. We also have two other girls, Morgan is thirteen, and Marilyn eleven. If I am correct, they are your grandchildren."

Ed held his breath and waited for the rest to come. He thought Gregory had a nice voice. As he continued his story in an even tone, he became self-assured: his voice stable, a man's voice.

"My wife realized how deeply I yearned to know who my father was, where I came from, whether I had siblings or not, and not only what medical history he might have had, but also what genes I might have inherited. I have three daughters and I wanted to make sure I did not give them the curse of some terrible disease. Sharon's Christmas present was a DNA testing kit and a membership to Genealogy.

"I know I was born in Hazelton, PA. Did you live there; let's say forty-two years ago? In the spring of 1978? If you did, did you happen to know my mother, Lula May Braxton? Petite, blonde, maybe twenty, and most likely drunk?"

"Sorry, Gregory, I have never lived in Hazelton. As a matter of fact, I have never lived in Pennsylvania. I lived in California, far from your place until I moved to the shores of the Atlantic, to Cecilia Beach, clear across the country. At the time of your birth, I still lived on the West Coast. And no, I cannot recall any woman by that name, either."

Gregory was clearly puzzled. "Then I don't understand how I was matched to you genetically. They tested me twice and both tests indicated you. How could they make a mistake?"

Ed interrupted him, "Wait a second. You said it was forty-two years ago? I was in Pennsylvania in 1978, at a conference. I believe it was in May. It was in the Split Rock Lodge. Not in Hazleton, but in Lake Harmony. Close enough. Oh, my, it just occurred to me, there was a little blonde in the bar. I swear, I would not be able to tell who approached the other. It might have been her, asking for matches. I just can't remember. Anyway, I picked up this girl, we had quite a few drinks, and then I took her out to my car. Gosh, I recall the little, yellow Volkswagen bug clearly. I can see the car in front of me much more than recalling her. Funny, but I don't think I knew her name even then. She staggered away soon. Anyway, I never had a chance to ask. Could that be your mother?"

"Most likely. I was born the following year at the end of February. May I ask you what you look like? Can you describe yourself?"

"Well, I am six-two, 242 lbs., have blonde hair, and blue eyes. My skin is white with red freckles. I used to be a businessman in a private firm, but sold my business and now I run a three-hundred-fifty bed hospital, though I am ready to retire next summer. About the hair, it's kind of thin, but it's there."

"Yes, you are like me, not much hair on the top here, either. And I am also in business. I graduated with an MBA from U-Penn and run my own company. It's not big, but it's mine. I started it and built it up to have twenty-five employees. You really could be my father. Do you have children?"

"We have four, but they are married and don't live with us. I live with my wife." After a little pause, he added: "Can we meet before I tell them? I want to be sure before I break the news to my family. It would naturally be a shock and I don't know how they will take it."

Gregory seemed to be pleased with the suggestion to meet him, because he eagerly replied. "Come to my home and meet my wife and daughters, too. We live in Jenkintown, near Philadelphia. When we hang up, I will text you the address. When do you want to visit?"

"I have a trip planned to Baltimore in two weeks. I could see you before I return."

"Perfect. Spend the weekend with us. Let's get acquainted. In my whole life I waited anxiously for meeting my father, but the next two weeks of waiting will be torture." He sounded sincere, Ed thought.

"Before I hang up the phone, may I ask you to do one more thing?" Gregory spoke softly now.

"Sure. Shoot. If I can, I will do it."

"Please call me Greg, Dad."

3

To err is human; to blame it on the other guy is even more human.

———

Bob Goddard

The statue of Saint Cecilia, the patron saint of the hospital, was removed from the façade when the city took over the care and management of the facility. Although officially it became Cecilia Beach Community Hospital, habits faded slowly and the old folks still referred to it by its previous name. Conversations were peppered with variations on the statement: "I stayed in Saint Cecilia for five whole days; my doctor said I had the worst case of migraine he had ever seen. I was an inch from the deathbed, for sure." Generations of families were born there, treated for various ailments, and died in Saint Cecilia.

Lately, the population of Cecilia Beach has changed. The once small beach community suddenly tripled in size. New buildings grew all over like mushrooms after rain. Developers took huge chunks of the nearby land to create fashionable gated communities. The price of real estate seemed to escalate and even the dilapidated, old beach homes sold for a premium price just to be torn down and be replaced by elaborate, sprawling mansions.

It certainly was a seller's market. Yet, buyers still flocked to Cecilia Beach and converted it into a booming city.

With the increased demand, the hospital added two new wings for a hundred-sixty extra beds and raised a new medical office building. Houses across the street were converted one after the other to medical offices, laboratories and some gave room to physical and respiratory therapies. Although they appeared to be independent facilities, the hospital owned and managed them all.

Ed Jamison's office was in the administrative wing. The conspicuous gold lettering on his door proudly announced he was a Ph.D. and the CEO of the entire Cecilia Beach Health System. He oversaw the development and operation of four hospitals and several free-standing clinics. He was a busy man, going from meetings to conferences, and carrying on day-long debates with contractors and vendors. People secretly whispered he would make deals with the Devil himself, if it was potentially beneficial for him. This morning he barely ended a heated discussion with the construction manager when his secretary connected the Dean of the Florida Medical School.

"Good morning, Dean. Sorry to bug you, but I need to know when the residents start their rotation. I was advised, it actually began last week. Do you know when the new resident, Siddiqui, can come? He was supposed to be here last Monday. You know, Bashir Siddiqui. The one with the perfect score."

"What do you mean, he is not there? He left the week before. He must be there. Give me five minutes. Let me check. I'll call you right back." Ed Jamison was friends with the Dean for a long time, but never heard him being as puzzled as now.

Ed got startled when the phone rang again. The Dean

of the faculty verified, Bashir Siddiqui was in Ed's hospital. Now it was Ed's turn to beg for time; he had to confirm what the head of the ICU reported the very morning: young Dr. Siddiqui had to testify in court on behalf of the University Hospital Emergency Department, and until the case was over, he was unable to start his rotation.

Finally, Ed and the Dean discovered the cause of the delay.

"So your star student, Dr. Siddiqui is somewhere in orbit, certainly not where he was supposed to be," Ed concluded.

The Dean was embarrassed, "Well, Siddiqui reported to us that he was in his new rotation at your hospital, but as I understood, he told you we held him back. A few months ago he was involved with an emergency room patient who sued us. True, he had to go for a deposition, but that was last week and lasted half a day only. We are investigating his whereabouts, trust me."

It took another week to discover Dr. Siddiqui had spent eleven days on the beach with a pretty, and rather promising, medical student. She was on break and she did not miss anything. Siddiqui, on the other hand, faced disciplinary actions from the school, and started on a very bad note in the hospital.

The rest of the day the CEO was filled with meetings. The much hoped for joint venture with the University Hospital came to nothing. Ed Jamison had to regroup in a hurry and changed his tactics by targeting others as potential saboteurs of the lucrative project. By directing a witch hunt, he hoped to survive the unexpected fiasco. Since this latest disappointment, he primarily focused on the extension of the hospital and the new Medical Arts Building. The deadline for ribbon-cutting was fast approaching. Every party pushed for a fast commencement: the physicians were just as eager to occupy the new offices as the hospital directors were excited to collect the rent for them. After all, the projected income should help with the expensive building project, for sure.

Before Ed left for the day, his secretary brought him the revised Baltimore itinerary. After his official business was over Friday noon, instead of flying directly back to Cecilia Beach, Ed took a weekend detour to Philadelphia.

"I have not seen some of my relatives in a long time. Perhaps this would be a good opportunity to rekindle the family ties." Ed casually explained his reason for changing his return ticket.

Sarah, his secretary, whole-heartedly supported the family trip, and appreciated his decision. "A family is everything. You never can ignore them. In the end, no one would stand by you, but the family. Not any of your friends, not your neighbors, and most certainly not your job. I bet your position would be advertised in the paper before you were even buried. Of course, you have to visit them. They are your family, and always would remain by you." She smiled approvingly as she left his office.

Ed's good mood soured as soon as Sarah reminded him of his family. So far, he had kept mum about the existence of Greg. He knew he had to face reality soon enough and come clean both to his wife and his children. Neither of it seemed to be an easy task.

He always considered his wife, Betty, a logical, but an emotionally distant person. Ed did not predict many fireworks after the revelation of a new son, but he was certain there would be plenty of sparks flying in every direction immediately afterward. He projected after a week or two of silent treatment that Betty would begin thawing the iceberg she had become and in about three months, all would return to normal. He just had to survive the few months of the cold war in a dog house.

He was much more worried about the rest of the family for he considered the children were less forgiving than his wife. After all, they were adults and did not depend on him anymore, unlike Betty, who led the comfortable life of a suburban housewife in relative luxury. Hearing the news the kids would more than likely gather around to protect their mother and condemn their father for cheating on her. The fact that he did it when their mother had young babies on her hands and when she sacrificed herself for them was absolutely unforgivable. Ed was convinced his daughter would never exonerate him, not the way she was. He eventually might find absolution from his sons, he thought. The devil, this crazy woman Sarah, she surely knew how to push his buttons by mentioning the word "family."

While Ed Jamison sweated the very thought of facing his wife and children, Sarah started to wrap up her present to the Board of Directors. Soon she was to deliver her boss to them. She planned to have him gift wrapped and delivered while declaring her concerns for the hospital and emphasizing her loyalty to the organization. She carefully avoided the slightest reference to her brief affair with Jamison. When Ed broke up their relationship, claiming his obligations to his wife, Sarah accepted his excuse. She no longer anticipated a quick divorce and a splendid wedding which she had pictured in her mind before. The love Ed claimed turned into ashes in her mouth and her thirst for revenge plundered her to a dark abyss. She swore she never would let Ed get away without being punished for her lost dreams.

As soon as she was alone at her desk Sarah made a new entry in her secret office diary she kept on her boss. Once completed, she placed the whole notebook into a large envelope. On her way home she planned to drop it in a mailbox.

4

Take your work seriously but yourself lightly.

C. W. Metcalf

As a charge nurse Josè got the first call on any admission, whether from the emergency room or a transfer within the hospital. The fifteen bed Intensive Care Unit was sufficient, although on a couple of occasions, they had to down-grade the least ill patient to make room for a newcomer.

At the beginning of his shift, Josè sat by the computer screen and read the history and treatment plan of the latest additions. The fifty-five-year-old Dave Cooper arrived shortly before midnight, and was diagnosed with an acute stroke. He showed up in the ER two days prior with dizziness and loss of balance. He was diagnosed with acute vertigo. A standard medication order was called into the Walmart pharmacy and he was instructed to pick it up on his way home. The next day he felt better and went to play golf with his friends. He got much worse on the golf course. His right leg became suddenly so feeble that it barely supported him, and he could not lift up his right arm. The others noted he slurred his words. His friends called 911, and an ambulance took him back to the ER.

Whatever happened there was not too clear to Josè. The chart was confusing, although it seemed the ER doctor did everything, including calling the University Hospital for a neuro interventionist to possibly remove a blood clot from the brain. The interventionist recommended the drug tissue plasminogen activator (tPA) instead. Dr. Ferguson did not agree with the recommendation and dictated in his note that it was his decision not to infuse the clot-busting medication. He wrote "the markedly elevated blood pressure and diabetes contradicted the use of tPA." He treated successfully the high blood pressure and gave two anti-thrombotic medications before he notified the neurologist on call.

Josè read the recorded conversation and approvingly bobbed his head seeing Dr. Redcliff corrected the ER physician. Josè always referred to the neurologist as a matter-of-fact, no-nonsense woman. "Just like a panty-hose," Dr. Redcliff responded to him laughingly.

"Darn it. She was right again. Diabetes was not one of the exclusion criteria for tPA. The blood pressure was controlled, so only the elapsed time and the administered drugs were contraindications." He turned to Betsy, the RN assigned to Mr. Cooper, "Good for Redcliff, she told Ferguson off."

"I think she simply stated the facts, I don't see any animosity, and do you?"

Josè quietly stared at the computer screen and pretended to be exceedingly busy to answer. Betsy was a good nurse but perhaps too good or too naive. Josè did not want to make an adversary.

"I called her for a consultation, but haven't seen her, yet. Have you?"

Betsy looked up. "Yes. Actually, I do. Right now. She just entered ICU."

"Good morning, ladies and gentlemen! Who do I

have to see?" Dr. Redcliff always had an upbeat voice and pleasant mannerism. Only her quick steps and wit were unexpected.

"Mr. Cooper in Bed 5. I am glad you are the 'stroke-ologist'. He needs you, trust me," Josè stated.

"May I tell you what's going on?" Betsy knew the vital signs, the CT scan and MRI reports, and all of the laboratory results. It was good to have her. She made the work easier.

"When you are finished with him, would you please take a couple of minutes to tell us what's going on?" The nurses all knew Dr. Redcliff was an RN before she decided to become a physician. The same background created comradery, and they felt comfortable asking her questions. She seemed to love teaching, anyway.

"Like I usually do? As part of the 'Five Minutes of Neurology' series by Dr. Redcliff? Gladly," Marsha agreed. "Come around when I talk to the family and especially when I review the MRI with them."

It took Dr. Redcliff an hour to go over the entire chart, interview Mr. Cooper, examine him thoroughly, order new tests, and dictate a two-page detailed summary. She sighed when Mrs. Cooper approached her. It took another half an hour to show her the MRI images on the computer screen and explain the findings in laymen's terms. By the end, Mrs. Cooper was so impressed and so comfortable with the neurologist that she hugged her. Dr. Redcliff was a bit embarrassed, but kept saying: "It was my pleasure."

As soon as Mrs. Cooper was out of hearing distance, Josè turned to Dr. Redcliff and whispered: "At least she thanked you, that's the most you could expect. You won't get a penny for this. They don't have any insurance."

"I already knew it, Josè." Dr. Redcliff looked at him with unwavering eyes. "I saw it on the chart. But he is ill, and I accepted him. See, how lucky I am to work for myself? Nobody can tell me what to do. The most I lose is my own time. Who is my other patient? I was called for another consultation for stroke-like symptoms."

"Bed 2, Mr. Winslow. Dr. Ramsey's nurse practitioner just saw him and ordered the neuro evaluation."

Dr. Redcliff turned and began to read the new patient's history. She was meticulous in reviewing every detail before facing a patient. She learned that this way no question had to be answered with a "Let me see, I didn't know about this." Suddenly she stopped in her steady progress, slightly shook her head as if clearing her sight, and scrolled back to the previous screen. "Josè, Mr. Winslow had elevated troponin level. Did you know that?"

"Yes, I saw it."

"Hmm. Is there an order for repeat testing? No? Then put one in for me, please. And repeat it in six, twelve, and twenty-four hours later. Thanks, Josè."

She sighed, and entered Mr. Winslow's room. In a few minutes she was absolutely sure the man had no stroke. He moved every limb with equal strength, his sensation was symmetrically intact, and even his speech was clear. He must have had a heart attack and the nurse practitioner missed it. Dr. Redcliff returned to the computer to enter her findings.

When she spotted Dr. Ramsey, she gave him report. "Dr. Ramsey, you run the ICU. Please check your nurse practitioner's note, I believe she did not realize Mr. Winslow had heart disease and not a stroke. I evaluated him. He did not have a stroke. His troponin level was quite high. I think he had a heart attack."

"You are very thorough, Dr. Redcliff. Thank you for letting me know. I will make the change in her dictation." Dr. Ramsey gave her a charming smile and disappeared.

She finished recording her findings. Before signing off, she skimmed over the nurse practitioner's progress note once more. In the interim, Dr. Ramsey co-signed the note. He made no change, wrote no new orders or additions. She shook her head in disbelief and ordered a cardiology consultation.

"Josè, I know it is not my job to get Mr. Winslow a cardiologist, but Dr. Ramsey knows about it. Would you please call Dr. Anthony to see patient in Bed 2 urgently?"

"Anything for you, Doc," Josè reached for the phone. "I will let Dr. Ramsey know when he gets back from lunch."

"Is it lunch time, already? Wow. I did not even notice how much time I've spent here."

"You may not have, but trust me, Dr. Ramsey did. You didn't look up but I saw how he rushed to get to the cafeteria before it was closed. He sure wouldn't miss a meal."

Marsha Redcliff pretended not to hear the last remark. She liked Dr. Ramsey, he seemed to be self-assured, radiated knowledge, and was extremely friendly. Actually, he was rather charming, and very good looking. The nurses all agreed he resembled Omar Sharif, just in an older version. Marsha had a chronic cough and needed periodic following after a nasty bout of pneumonia which landed her in the hospital. Her shortness of breath rapidly worsened so they took her to the operating room to clear the mucus plugs from her lung. After this experience, she needed a good pulmonologist. When she heard Dr. Ramsey graduated from the same residency program where she spent her miserable internship, she decided to ask him to be her doctor.

Although she was annoyed by Dr. Ramsey's current indifference, she realized they had to work together. He was the head of Internal Medicine, and being a neurologist, Marsha belonged to his department. He also was a born charmer, always complimentary, and in spite of a huge patient load both in the hospital and in his booming private practice, he found time to chat with anyone.

Marsha liked him, yet, somewhere deep inside, she felt as if he slimed her after each of their encounters. She brushed aside the bad feelings soon, because Dr. Ramsey was easy to get along with, and highly complementary to her. In spite of maintaining close contact, their relationship remained professional, and they kept addressing each other by their full name and title. Marsha felt the best was to keep a friendly distance because Dr. Ramsey was one of the "good old boys" in the hospital hierarchy.

She decided, no harm was done anyway, she caught the omission. In the elevator she bumped into the cardiologist and told him of her suspected diagnosis. Dr. Anthony was already heading to ICU to visit Mr. Winslow. She quickly added: "Thanks for coming immediately. Once you are done with him, would you mind stopping at Mr. Cooper, Bed 5, too? He had multiple strokes, all in the left brain; I suspect an embolic cause. His carotid ultrasound was clean so it must originate from his heart. He would benefit from your evaluation, Dr. Anthony." The cardiologist agreed.

She left with the good feeling of being effective, useful, and knowledgeable. No nagging sensation of something being missed. She knew she did her best and gave her most. By taking care of her patient's body and soul, she attended the whole patient, not only the isolated neurological problems. She gave total care, focusing on neurology, yet, not missing the other diseases. The way she always wanted to function as a physician: Dr. Marsha Redcliff, Medicine Woman.

5

*We know what a person thinks not when he tells
us what he thinks, but by his actions.*

———

Isaac Bashevis Singer

Marsha lived alone. Her immunologist husband married her when she was a nurse, and divorced her as soon as she became a neurologist. He clearly resented the fact that his wife had become a physician. He graduated forty years prior, and although he was adequate in his job, he slowly got obsolete by not keeping up with the new discoveries. His wife's recent graduation and especially becoming Resident of the Year irritated him. He no longer could pull rank over her.

After the bitter divorce they never talked again. When lawyers get involved in an amicable divorce, all end up as enemies. Marsha supported herself the same as before, and since her husband never shared finances with her, nothing changed much. She just added a huge mortgage to her expenses and did one less load of laundry. Life went on and it was good.

Her role in raising two children ended when they earned their degrees and met their spouses at the university. They never returned home except for rare and short visits. Marsha accepted it as a natural course of life. After all, children were given to the parents on a loan and only for their formative years. Still, she felt they were her highest accomplishment and felt lucky to be entrusted with their upbringing.

She owned her home only on paper. She lived in it, but the truth was her finance company was the legal home owner. The newly built house had white walls and off-white carpeting which made the whole inside look fatally anemic. It took her a couple of years to get the courage and money to change the color scheme. Needless to say, the warm earth and sun colors of the freshly painted walls made a cheerful difference. Eventually, a new hardwood floor replaced the anemic carpet. She called her home the "House of Sunshine." Every month she spent her salary on ensuring her approaching retirement was comfortable and nice. Her family jokingly labeled this as "feathering the nest."

After working for three years for the Cecilia Beach Medical Group, she resigned and was forced to get a job in another county. Her contract stipulated a strict geographic restriction and for two years she could not take another position in the vicinity. In the entire county, all hospitals were owned by the Cecilia Beach system, and once someone left an employment in one of their facilities, the monopoly effectively prevented re-employment in the vicinity. The final offer came with almost doubling her salary, but it was six hours away. She closed up the "House of Sunshine", rented a small apartment near her new hospital, and worked sixty hours a week. Three years later, shortly after New Year, her neighbor's late-night call gave her a shock.

"Marsha, this is Debbie. I have bad news for you. Your patio screen was slashed open, and your glass panel was smashed on your back door. Someone broke in. I called the police. They have just arrived and are investigating the damage. They asked me to notify you."

"What the... I can't believe it! When did it happen?"

"We noticed your screen door was open so I went over to close it. That's when I saw the broken glass. Listen, I have to go, the police have some questions. I think you should get back as soon as you can."

"I am six hours away, but I will leave immediately. Tell the police I should be there by dawn."

Marsha realized the best defense of a home was a live-in owner. She resigned from her job, and the next month she was back in Cecilia Beach. She opened her Neurology Clinic and thrived as a private practitioner. Sometimes accidents mean salvation.

The loud ring of her cell phone brought her back to reality. She was on-call for the hospital; she could not ignore her phone. Why should she? What happened was in the past. It was a done deal. Unless she wanted to get upset again or learn from it some lessons, it was useless to re-live it. Why look back? It was not the direction she was heading. Let's deal with the current problems for each day brings enough misery at the doorstep.

"Dr. Redcliff? It's Betsy from ICU. Sorry to bother you, but Mr. Cooper is complaining of blurred vision. He also has more facial tingling. His vitals are fine. Nothing else has changed."

"Thanks, Betsy. Send him to CT STAT. CT of the brain, no contrast, now, and call me with the result. I am on my way, should be there by the time he is back in his bed."

An hour later Marsha was back at the computer screen, explaining to Mrs. Cooper that according to the images, the stroke has enlarged. Whether this was an additional new focus or the old one got worse, no one knew. The CT was not sensitive enough to tell. She needed to order a repeat MRI.

As she talked to the crying woman, it occurred to her that swelling of the brain also could have caused the symptoms. The insult was two days old, but if she considered the prior ER visit, and perhaps erroneous diagnosis of vertigo, it started four days prior. Surely, by this time swelling could have developed in the area.

"A stroke occurs at once, not over several days, piece-meal style". She almost heard the lecturer's voice from her long past residency. In that case it was a recurrence, most likely multiple strokes, she decided. It had to be embolic. Thank Heaven, Dr. Anthony was involved already. Indeed, by the end of the day, he diagnosed Mr. Cooper with periodic, irregular heartbeat which showered his brain with clots. He started anticoagulation.

The new MRI confirmed Marsha's suspicion: swelling put extra pressure on the nerves causing partial vision loss and sensory changes. The use of an osmotic diuretic for brain edema was not frequently used in the community hospital. The pharmacist questioned her order, but when she explained to him the reason, he quickly agreed. In a few hours clear vision returned, and the facial tingling disappeared. She diagnosed the problem correctly: the proof was in the reaction to the drug.

Cecilia Beach Community Hospital had no neuro-surgical service. Assistance was offered by the nearby University Hospital, and patients usually were rapidly transferred if the need arose. After several phone calls, Mr. Cooper was accepted, and the following morning left the hospital for the university.

"Dr. Redcliff, you did a terrific job", the neurosurgeon complimented her. "I just wish the ER would have followed my recommendations. Then I wouldn't have to face the music now. Anyway, thanks, we'll take care of Mr. Cooper from here on, don't worry."

Dr. Ramsey cheerfully greeted her and casually

mentioned "By the way, old Winslow had a massive heart attack. Good, *we* called a cardiologist."

Marsha rolled her eyes and replied; "We? Indeed, it was good." But Ramsey already passed her, followed by his shadow, Dr. Siddiqui, Josè, and a couple of nurses. If he heard Marsha, he showed no reaction, whatsoever. Recently Dr. Ramsey reincarnated the medical teaching rounds, exactly as they all experienced when they were interns and residents. Today and here he was the professor: infallible, his knowledge was not to be questioned. All around him were to take his statements as if he were Moses, descending from Mount Sinai with the Ten Commandments.

The rest of the day she read electroencephalograms on the second floor, evaluated patients on the third floor, rushed to the ER, and then returned to repeat the same all over. She did not have time to get lunch, and missed dinner, too. She made a cup of hot tea and grabbed two crackers from the ICU lounge. She laughed when Josè questioned her which cracker was for lunch and which was for dinner. He offered her a stick of chewing gum, "In case you want dessert, too."

When she got home, the usual gratifying feeling greeted her as soon as she entered the "House of Sunshine". It was good to kick off her high heels and finally eat some food. Before she retired to her bedroom, she reviewed the article she wrote. She made a couple of corrections in the punctuation and then with one push of a button, posted it on her website to be seen by everyone.

Sense of Entitlement

When I was a child, I thought everything was naturally there for my well-being: my parents, the home, food, clothes, and toys. I have learned the hard way later how much I had to work to get everything. No more freebies. Nothing came easy or fast, but eventually I succeeded.

Maybe my own experience makes the current trend of unrealistic demands and sense of entitlement so unpalatable for me. Frivolously using terms of "racism", "misogyny", "xenophobia", "supremacist", "fascist", "Hitlerian", "Stalinist", "socialism", and the Good Lord knows what else doesn't strengthen necessarily a position in a dialogue. Quite contrarily, it shows inherent weakness, inability to discuss a disagreement in a civilized manner, lacking tools to argue, and poor vocabulary skills. Add to it an overwhelming sense of entitlement and the communication breakdown is complete.

As you gathered, I am a physician. I have 29 years of education, two Bachelor's degrees (BS and BA), a Master's degree (MSN), and an MD behind my name. I worked myself up from being a legal immigrant with five workable English words (car, sandwich, cocktail, movie star, and kiss) through being an RN, then an ARNP, then a PA-C, and finally a physician with four years of residency and an extra year of fellowship in neurology. I was named Resident of the Year at the Neurology Program and got numerous awards for my excellent patient care afterward. Of course, I have learned English. I paid during the early years and paid dearly: not only accumulating a tremendous financial burden, but keeping my nose in the books and depriving myself of any luxuries. I went to no or maybe one to two parties altogether, no movies, nothing but text books, no breaks. And I ate more Ramen noodles and Philadelphia soft pretzels than I care to remember.

Being Board certified, I am called a "stroke-ologist" and also see general neuro patients in two hospitals. A week ago, I was called to evaluate a fifty-two year-old man who had no insurance and expected every possible intervention. He had an ER MD evaluation, an internist's admission, and then I was called. By that time he had umpteen labs, a chest X-ray, and a head CT. I ordered an MRI and MRA of the head, because he could have had a midbrain lesion or stroke since both of his eyes recently deviated to the sides and to his temples.

He volunteered to assure me of not paying a penny because, "you are a doctor, and have enough money. I am a specialized car mechanic, but I could not afford to pay for insurance." He smoked a pack and a half of cigarettes per day ($270 a month), and drank half pack of beer per day ($120 a month), more on the weekends.

I could not afford such luxuries with all my bills (malpractice, hospital privileges, office overhead, NICA, ANA, AMA, various medical licenses, mandatory continuing education, etc.) and I got the big bucks? He partied and lived high while I ate Ramen noodles and studied. Now he compares apples with oranges and thinks it is fair or just to expect total care totally free?

I asked him, being a car mechanic, would he repair a car knowing he never would see a penny for his work? His answer was a very honest, "Hell, no." I smiled, and replied as pleasantly as I could, "See, this is the difference. I do everything for you the same as if I were paid." It took over an hour to complete the workup, make arrangements for him to see outside help, and teach him what to look for and what to avoid in the future. And, I managed to smile and be pleasant during the entire time.

Before departing, he gave me another doozy: "Can you order a *complete body* MRI? I thought, since I am here, I might as well get it done free."

So where is this entitlement coming from???

Furthermore, am I to pay for it???

Almost instantly someone replied with an "Amen" comment.

6

The treacherous, unexplored areas of the world are not in continents or the seas; they are in the minds and hearts of men.

———

Allen E. Claxton

The morning teaching rounds started off on shaky legs, but now they progressed smoothly. Dr. Ramsey was glad he initiated it. He patterned the rounds after the ones he participated in as a resident, although it seems eons ago. The difference was that this time he no longer was picked on but was the one who asked the questions. He carefully chose his topics because, in case no one knew what the correct answer was, he had to give all the explanations.

On Dr. Siddiqui's first round he almost lost face when the young doctor easily quoted all the numbers and statistical outcome of a study. He evidently knew more about it than Dr. Ramsey. Ever since that embarrassing close call, he looked up an article in his medical journal the night before, and only after he thoroughly educated himself on the topic, did he dare to choose it to be discussed. In the morning he cleverly included it into the teaching routine by making a casual reference to the article. The rest of patient care related information and management were standard care. In the end, he convinced himself, as well as all around him, that Cecilia

34

Beach Community Hospital was on the same level as any medical school.

Young Dr. Siddiqui's obvious vast medical knowledge impressed everyone.

"It was clear that he read every printed word of a textbook, cover to cover, including the dedication, and most likely who the printing company was, too," Josè declared.

"Did you hear he had perfect scores on every test while in med school?" Dr. Ramsey proudly announced to everyone. Dr. Siddiqui's persistent perfect test scores intimidated his coworkers, and made him the star pupil of his proud professors. After all, his stellar records reflected on his instructors, didn't they? The initial mishap surrounding his late start was quickly forgotten, and they all looked up to him with respect and slight intimidation.

Everyone, but Dr. Redcliff. Not that she knew nearly as much of, let's say, biochemistry as Dr. Siddiqui, but she researched every reference made to her and predictably returned as a well-trained family ghost with additional information. In other words, she was a royal pain.

Way before the morning rounds started, Dr. Redcliff sat by the computer getting familiar with her new patients. Her inquiry of "Who was following Mr. Castro in Bed 1?" didn't stop Josè in his routine. He just replied without turning his head "Dr. Siddiqui."

"Dr. Siddiqui, may I see you?"

"Of course, Dr. Redcliff. What can I do for you?" Siddiqui was always smooth and agreeable.

"Could you tell me what's going on with Mr. Castro?"

"Of course. He is an eighty-two-year old Hispanic male with hypertension, uncontrolled diabetes mellitus, dyslipidemia, coronary artery disease, status post three stent placements, and significant non-compliance. He was admitted with a transient ischemic attack. He also has a degenerative joint disease, early dementia, and visual hallucinations." Bashir Siddiqui radiated certainty. His memory never failed him, yet.

"That's fine, but tell me what happened to him over the weekend." Dr. Redcliff seemed to pursue her original idea; obviously the list of diagnoses was not what she wanted to hear.

"He became DNR and comfort care as of Friday. I got the forms to the family, myself. Hospice is following him now. He is no longer our concern."

"Do me a favor Dr. Siddiqui, find me the signed 'Do Not Resuscitate' copy in his chart." Marsha Redcliff's voice was even-toned and pleasant.

Bashir Siddiqui picked up the patient's chart and was determined to shut this annoying neurologist up by shoving the requested form into her face. Except the form was missing. He went through the paper chart twice, page by page, and it was not there.

"I don't understand it. I personally explained to them what the DNR meant, where they had to sign the form, and instructed them to give it to the charge nurse." Siddiqui was baffled to say the least.

"I see. Josè, do you have the form?" Dr. Redcliff turned to the charge nurse.

"No."

"How come?"

"The family decided not to make him DNR, after all."

Marsha Redcliff turned to the resident, "So you signed off on his care prematurely, didn't you?" Although her words were intended as a question, they sounded like an accusation to everyone.

"After you assumed the family signed the permit, you further assumed hospice took over, and you were off the hook. But hospice was never notified, because they did not need to be called. So who saw the patient on

Saturday and Sunday? No one. He had nursing care but nothing else." Redcliff's voice was cold and each word dropped with the clear sound of crashing ice as if it were hail during a fast-moving summer hailstorm.

"Please see the weekend lab results, now." Dr. Redcliff's voice became ominous.

"I already did, just in case, and they were all right." Dr. Siddiqui started to regain his confidence once more. Obviously, he tried to save the sinking ship.

"Then do it again. Now." The provoked Siddiqui thought Redcliff just couldn't give up.

All the nurses gathered around them, quietly looking at the screen as Dr. Siddiqui quickly scrolled over the labs. Suddenly he stopped and his facial arrogance changed into a mixture of fear and surprise.

"So you did not see the labs before, right?" Dr. Redcliff watched Siddiqui's face. "Otherwise you could not tell me, 'they were all right' could you? They were far from being alright, because he had a massive heart attack on Saturday night. You thought Mr. Castro's family would follow your instructions and sign the DNR, then get hospice for him, but they didn't. You never checked back with them. You just signed off on him. Wrote him off, didn't you? You told me you reviewed his labs. You didn't. Tell me, how can I trust you again?" Dr. Redcliff's glare remained on Siddiqui's face.

"He has multiple organ diseases and dementia. He is going soon, anyway." Siddiqui did not seem to be perturbed.

"That is not your or my decision to make: certainly not a reason to withdraw care. Who do you think you were, God?" Dr. Redcliff clearly was indignant. "Tell me, is that how your mother raised you? Aren't you ashamed?"

Dr. Siddiqui could not think what to say for the first time in his life.

Dr. Redcliff continued: "From now on you are to review every patient's every lab and test results every morning. The ICU is never full so you have plenty of time to do it. Be ready to give me a report before you start morning rounds with Dr. Ramsey."

"I will, as long as there are not too many patients."

Siddiqui was humiliated. He was not going to allow this woman to treat him like a greenhorn intern. He graduated with every honor, got the highest scores on his board examination, and all he had to complete was this final rotation of miserable few weeks in this crummy little community hospital. Once this was over, he would get his license and accept a teaching position somewhere in a faculty of an Ivy League medical school. He was on his way to freedom.

The flip answer and impertinence angered Dr. Redcliff. She sternly replied, "You will do it," and she put extra emphasis on the word 'will.' "You will even if every ICU bed is occupied and extra patients are piled up in the hallway. This is when you come in early and leave late. End of discussion." She turned to Josè with an order to consult Dr. Anthony immediately. She ignored the idly standing Dr. Siddiqui who eventually retreated.

In the afternoon Dr. Ramsey approached her with Dr. Siddiqui's grievance. "I am disturbed by Dr. Siddiqui's complaints, Dr. Redcliff. He said you were very demanding and humiliated him in front of everyone. What happened?"

Marsha Redcliff was incredulous. Bashir Siddiqui dared to protest to his preceptor after he ignored a patient, missed two days of care, and an acute disease development. On top of it all, he covered his involvement with a lie. He truly was shameless.

She quickly described what happened then concluded: "I have my concerns of Dr. Siddiqui being a physician. Not of his book knowledge, because obviously he has that. But he has not one iota of care or a grain of compassion. His heart is not in his profession. Furthermore, he cheats and lies to cover his mistakes. I understand he did the same before, yet, he did not learn from being reprimanded. This is dangerous. This is unacceptable behavior. You have to notify his medical school."

The bartering continued for a while. To Dr. Ramsey's calming and unmistakably protective approach, Marsha Redcliff responded with a quick: "Would you like to have him as your mother's or child's doctor?"

Dr. Ramsey soothingly replied to his indignant colleague: "Can you give him a little slack? I know you are very good at what you do, meticulous and caring. But, my dear Dr. Redcliff, think of the many years you developed yourself to be what you are. Dr. Siddiqui probably had the first real-life encounter in a hospital setting and did not handle it well. I grant you that much. But we all know he is smart. I am sure he learned a big lesson and never would forget what you thought him today. Can you work with him in the next few weeks and teach him to improve? You only have to share the neuro patients with him, I am responsible for the rest."

Gosh, he was smooth, thought Marsha. *Now I know why he was the head of the department. Seemingly he agreed with me while defending Siddiqui. And, in the end, he put me in my place. Be cautious Marsha,* she told herself, *Ramsey's oily smooth diplomacy not only has a smile but a bite, too.*

"Certainly. The problem is that no matter how much you do, you cannot give him a heart. As long as he does his job and doesn't forget what I said to him, I certainly can work with him. You said, we only share the neuro patients."

The next month passed with very little else but hard

work. Dr. Ramsey kept praising his protégée, and Dr. Siddiqui kept a low profile when Marsha was around. The day after his license arrived, he left the hospital. Dr. Ramsey organized a small luncheon in the ICU lounge for him. Each nurse contributed by bringing a dish, a salad or a dessert. Dr. Ramsey ordered a huge cake with "Congratulations to Our Best Resident" written on top among the gaudy, colorful, flower border. Aside this, by all measures, it was a lovely day. There were only a few patients in ICU and intense comradery flowed abundantly.

By the evening Dr. Ramsey's upset and raised voice splintered the upbeat spirit: half of his textbooks disappeared from his bookshelves. No one could prove Dr. Siddiqui took them, although all saw he carried out several boxes from the hospital. From that day on Dr. Ramsey locked his office door, and never mentioned Siddiqui's perfect scores again.

Marsha Redcliff bit her tongue not to say a word to her furious colleague. She thought Karma paid back everything with interest to Dr. Ramsey for being blindly impressed by Siddiqui's book knowledge. Her observation of the resident's lack of conscience and character was proven. In spite of his perfect scores he was nothing but an unscrupulous, self-serving, and shallow individual. Nothing but an educated bum... really. That was enough validation for her.

She was convinced that one day she would hear about Dr. Siddiqui again. It probably will be either in the medical journal praising his novel therapy of some previously untreatable disease or in the daily news for killing a patient.

7

Listen, or thy tongue will keep thee deaf.

———

Native American Proverb

Marsha Redcliff had her yearly evaluation for chronic cough. Dr. Ramsey ordered a repeated chest X-ray, but changed the order to a CT scan at Marsha's request. A month later, just before the Christmas holidays started, his nurse practitioner saw Marsha.

"Nothing has changed on your recent CT scan. It's OK. It only confirmed the already diagnosed bronchiectasis," she assured her.

"Are you sure this causes my coughing spells? Is it the correct diagnosis? Because if the diagnosis and the recommended treatment were correct, the coughing should have stopped long ago. One or the other must be wrong. Lately, my cough intensified and also became a bit productive."

The nurse practitioner did not look up from her writing. Marsha continued, "It really is embarrassing because it catches me off guard, and I cannot stop coughing for twenty minutes. Do you realize what it means when everyone around you stops talking and looks at you expecting to stop the cough so they could resume the discussion? It's really mortifying. Like they were expecting me to spit out the lung or something," Marsha complained.

"Are you using your inhalers three or four times a day?"

"None. They are just as efficient as Voodoo would be. They are totally useless, and they only give me a bad after-taste. As a matter of fact, they seem to trigger my coughing spells."

Marsha was too tired to repeat to her what she already said to Dr. Ramsey: neither the inhalers nor the intermittent pressure vest therapy helped her. The inhalers actually made her cough more. It seemed as if they were incepting the spells.

The nurse practitioner sighed and recommended a cough syrup. "This should help, but this time take it please. You know, it's like birth control pills: they only work when you take them." She offered her a prescription.

Marsha was indignant. No one listened to her. On her last visit, she complained of the same to Dr. Ramsey. He did not change her medications, only ordered a CT scan and disappeared. For the follow-up visit he sent his nurse practitioner to see Marsha. The nurse excused the absence of her boss by claiming, "He was busy with other patients – you know the really sick ones who needed his specialized expertise." Apparently, Dr. Ramsey got convinced that a bit of coughing could be easily managed by his assistant.

Now Marsha found herself reasoning with an even less educated person. She felt frustrated and the rising anger further irritated her. She only calmed down, recalling Dr. Ramsey monopolized the greater beach area being the only pulmonary specialist with all six similarly educated doctors working for him. Where else could she go? At least Dr. Ramsey was a colleague and as such he should treat her with more care than a completely strange specialist somewhere in the next county.

"Trust me, I realize there is no free lunch, each drug has its side effects. I know the cough syrup would put me to sleep. I could not, and should not, function while taking it. I am a physician and know what I am talking about." Marsha was indignant.

Hycodan was a medication which would have suppressed her cough but also would have put her to sleep. How could she function as a physician if she was not alert? She should not even sit behind a steering wheel while being on the drug, let alone make life altering decisions.

She shook her head, "No, don't give me any cough syrups. I don't want to treat only the symptoms and not the underlying cause."

The nurse practitioner laughingly brushed off her irritation by saying, "Yep, I see what Dr. Ramsey said. You are a doctor, and that means you are not a good patient."

In the end nothing changed in her care. The nurse practitioner assured her all was under control, but sternly instructed her to keep using the inhaler, and return in one year for follow-up. In full self-appreciation she added, "Of course you know to call us sooner if any problem would occur. I am here to take care of you." Marsha silently wished the woman would go away to a deserted island.

On her way back to the hospital, memories of her encounters with various physicians flooded her mind. In her last job as an RN she worked for the Tumor Registry at Drexler University in Philadelphia. She had great autonomy in her job, and ample opportunity to read about solid tumors. She still could virtually see the faded red cover of the Rochester University's oncology book she used for reference material. She had the joy to learn about interesting new diseases and novel therapies. She was an RN then but also a "wannabe" physician. The more she read the more she liked pulmonary medicine. She decided that if she ever had a chance to become an MD she would like to be a lung cancer doctor. The Drexler medical staff encouraged her to pursue her dream. Unfortunately, her situation was complicated with two small children and a bad marriage. It took a burning desire to commit herself to seven or eight years of studying.

One of her preceptors was Dr. Franklin Stone, a nationally respected authority on miner's black lung disease and tuberculosis. He noted her prolonged cough after a bout of bronchitis and recommended testing. Her pulmonary function was normal, but the X-ray showed a possible old infection. The rest of her tests were all negative. After much contemplation, Dr. Stone put her on a year and half of antibacterial therapy for an old TB exposure. His words took on a serious tone as he explained the prophylaxis, "You probably have very little chance to get a recurrence, but a TB bacillus is sneaky and lives forever walled up in its little cocoon. As you get older, your immunity will fall and the bacillus may breakthrough and cause havoc. Better be afraid now then be frightened later. Besides, I am selfish, I want to employ you once you graduate." A totally unexpected heart attack killed Dr. Stone two weeks after her graduation.

Her new pulmonologist at Drexler tried every pill, every inhaler without one iota change in her condition. After the specialist almost missed the targeted biopsy area, his patience ran out. He sent her away with the good wish of "May you cough for another thirty years. I have no idea what's wrong with you."

Shortly after the pulmonary doctor's discharge, her neurology professor called her into his office and diagnosed her with a nervous cough. He recommended Marsha to work at suppressing the cough conscientiously,

"Because", in his opinion, "It was already embedded as a pattern in your mind. It is purely psychogenic in origin."

That's when she suddenly saw her professor in a new light and lost respect for him. He fell off from the imaginary pedestal she placed him on, completely, totally, and irrevocably. Rather than seeing him as an idol, now she only saw a man of retirement age who thought he knew everything. She did not exonerate him completely, though she realized the teaching position gave him the false security of infallible knowledge. Ultimately, facing students every day convinced him of being an expert not only in his own but in every area of medicine.

Marsha never uttered a word of response to her professor, because she recalled her late father's warning: "Always remember you never can win against a teacher or a judge. Just look agreeable and walk away." That's precisely what she did.

Marsha felt at unease to be shoved to the nurse practitioner's care instead of being seen by the physician. After the office visit, she was angry with herself for not speaking up, to remain quiet. She felt something was definitely wrong with her; either the diagnosis or the treatment was inaccurate. Supposedly she was given the best possible care by a nurse practitioner, who had a one-year, watered-down, general medicine added to a nursing background. That did not sound very assuring. She knew first-hand the extensive depth of medicine she had to learn in medical school after being a nurse practitioner, herself. Later she became the preceptor for nurse practitioner students and saw the superficiality of their learning. Furthermore, even common courtesy to a fellow professional should have prevented her to be sent to a lesser educated caregiver. Apparently, Dr. Ramsey had no qualms about his colleague being treated by a nurse.

Lately, Dr. Ramsey and his nurse practitioner both expressed their opinion of all was under control while they were in charge of her care. Marsha hardly believed them because she kept coughing as prior but recognized she was a neurologist and not a board-certified lung specialist; therefore, she should listen to those who were better qualified to do the job. She should return to the subject of neurology, what was her area of expertise.

In the interim, she arrived at the hospital and entered to pick up her assignment for the day. Dr. Pacheco, the other neurologist, had a day-off and left Marsha a list of her patients to follow, too. Seeing the two-page list of patients waiting to be seen, she decided to do the new evaluations first then visit the follow-ups. Her personal problems faded away as she concentrated only on those who needed her help.

8

To carry a grudge is like being stung to death by one bee.

William H. Walton

Ed Jamison left his luggage in the hallway and rushed to greet his wife. He tried to be attentive and loving, but his gut was in knots, realizing he faced the awful task of telling her about the newly discovered son. Although he was certain it would be a very uncomfortable evening, but even in his wildest imagination, he did not project the outcome.

"How was your trip? Did you accomplish everything?" asked his wife as she served dinner.

"Oh, yes, it went well. You know me; I always can negotiate a good deal." Ed tried his hardest to remain calm and composed. He didn't want to give her any reason to be upset prematurely.

"Yep, you have the gift of gab, alright."

"No dear, it really is an art to lead any discussion in the direction you want to, and ultimately end up with the results you desire. In reality, negotiation is nothing but a chess game." Ed appeared to placate his wife. "My secretary made the itinerary and scheduled me with back-to-back meetings. I had no time for anything else."

She remained silent for a long time and kept stirring her food slowly with her fork before she asked: "How about your private business? Do you want to talk about that?"

"What private business?" Ed looked up. "Where did you get this idea?"

"Come, come, Ed, I know you better than you think. You took casual clothes which you never wear for a business meeting. Did you carry out business negotiations on Friday evening? How about Saturday and Sunday? Do you think I am dumb and completely blind? Your bimbo secretary, Sarah, called from your office. When I told her you were not home yet, she apologized. She pretended to forget about your weekend trip. Huh, likely story. I bet she just wanted to let me know you went to Philadelphia."

"Oh that, I wanted to discuss that side trip with you in detail. By the way, I got you something there. Did you know Philadelphia had a jewelry row in Center City? I saw it in a window and thought of you. Isn't this the kind of ring you have always wanted?" He gave her a small jewelry box. Betty opened it to expose a sparkling diamond ring.

"Thank you, Ed. It is very similar to the one I had always wanted. It certainly is beautiful." She did not seem to be overwhelmed by the present, though apparently, she liked it.

"Beautiful? It is almost two carats! Of course, it is beautiful." Ed was indignant though only cautiously showing his disappointment. *Nothing out of the ordinary behavior,* he kept repeating to himself. Women had the extra sense and uncanny ability to pick up tiny signals indicating otherwise. "I thought you would like it, or at least you would be impressed by the size of the stone, if nothing else."

"The bigger the sin, the bigger the diamond," replied Betty in a flat tone. She left the box on the kitchen counter and turned to Ed, "Tell me about your side trip first."

"That's what I wanted to do. Wait until you hear the whole thing. You wouldn't believe it. Grab your glass of wine; let's sit by the pool and talk about it."

Once settled in the slowly growing shadows of the palm trees, Ed told her the shocking news from the astounding phone call to the visit at his new son's home. He downplayed the trip stating he did not want to unnecessarily upset the family unless he was convinced of the truth of what Greg said. Ed watched his wife sitting rigidly in her chair, with her face covered by the shadows. She stirred after a long and uncomfortable pause, "So now you are convinced this man is your son, am I right?"

"Betty you should see him. He looks like me forty years ago. A spitting image of me. He is successful, has a nice family, and beautiful daughters. All of them are blonde, have big blue eyes, and are really sweet. Good students, impeccable manners. You would definitely like them."

"No, thanks, Ed. I have my, that is *our*, four children. They are enough for me." Betty's voice was cold and measured. "What else? Anything else I should know?"

"I told you everything." He expectantly watched her rigid body, as she sat with a straight back, arms crossed at her waist, and legs crossed beneath her. He realized this is what the body language experts called "closing in" or "locked-in" position. Maybe she wanted to block the news. Actually, he thought she took the news better than he expected. He truly anticipated a big fight ensuing his initial announcement, but Betty was level headed and distant, as always. He hoped that after a few days in a dog house, all would return to the normal way of living. They gained a couple of new family members that's all. She'll get used to it.

"Really? You told me everything. No, not everything. Tell me when and how it happened."

"Do you remember when I went to a conference in Pennsylvania? The one where you were supposed to accompany me, but you altered your mind at the very last minute, remember?

"Yes, I remember it, and I remember it well. So that's when you picked up the floozy. Did I understand you properly? You blamed me for your philandering? Was it my fault that you never could keep your zipper up? Was it? Oh, I know more about you than what you really think. You are utterly shameless. But no, it's not enough crime for you to cheat on your wife; you have to pile more sins on top of it. Because that's what you did by attempting to portray me as the cause of your transgressions. And you think it's just and right for me to pay for it. Let me tell you, Ed Jamison, if anyone will pay, it will be you. Because if you think for a second that your new son does not know how much money you have and how much he could inherit at the end, you are absolutely wrong."

"I don't believe it, Betty. You don't know him. He is not that kind."

"I don't know him, but you do? Isn't it amazing? Out of the clear blue sky he calls you once, you get together for two days, and now you have an unbreakable father-son relationship. Aren't you being just a trifle bit too gullible?"

"What I mean is that he does not need my money. He has his own corporation and makes a good living. He has a nice home, posh location, two nice cars. What else would he need from me? He just wants to have his father. He never had a father before. Can't you understand this?"

"I can. What I can't understand is that: why can't you treat your own children alike? You could go to visit a complete stranger because he claims to be your son but not your own son who lives two hours away. Fine father you are!"

"Betty, you know I love my children. I would do anything for them."

"Anything? Like what? You cheated on me before and now you are cheating on them. Just hold your horses, don't interrupt me. You just stole one-fifth of their inheritance. You robbed them. If you die, whatever you leave will go to five, instead of four people. Is not that cheating them? Don't you think I see what you are doing?"

"Betty, why are you harping on the inheritance; am I to die soon? Do you know something I don't?"

"I don't harp on anything. Thank you for the compliment. I only say it because, you are getting old. Open your eyes and look in the mirror once. You have a potbelly. You have a bad heart. Your blood pressure and cholesterol levels are dangerously high, and so is your weight. You can keel over at any moment. Don't you think your beloved new son would not claim his share the minute he hears you kicked the bucket?"

"Oh, my God! You are crazy!" Ed got agitated. He felt dizzy and realized his blood pressure must be climbing steadily. He conscientiously forced himself to calm down. No, Betty should not get him ill, although clearly that's what she was aiming to do. Money, money, money. The root of all evil. That's all what matters to her. Always had and always will.

"Yeah, I am crazy. I sure must be to stay with you for forty-five years, raise your four children, and take care of you. I am the one who is crazy. Then what are you? Who are you? Do I even know you?" Betty's words sputtered with venom.

"I am the man who married you, the husband who tolerated your family as your sister and your brother-in-law steadily replaced me. The cuckold who secured your life with whatever you wanted. I gave you a life that you only could hope to get. You never had to work a day of your life. You got a maid, a gardener, and only the good Lord knows what else. I gave you everything, all that you had ever wanted."

"So raising four children is not hard? Thanks a lot. I knew you were a lousy father, but now, I have realized, you were a lousy husband, too. You sold your business to stack the profit away. Did I spend a penny from it? No, I didn't. You went to work for the hospital for a title and for much less money, because you wanted to be the CEO. Did I object? No, I didn't. Can a fat savings account make up for that? I guess, it can work for you. Let's face it. The sole reason for being a housewife was that someone needed to provide you with a clean and comfortable home, not because I wanted it." Her words hit him like a whip; he could not get away or interject a word into the escalating tirade.

Betty acridly continued, "You have never been faithful to me, I know it now. My sister warned me so many times, but I did not want to believe her. Now you proved it to me. There is no better way to do it than telling the unsuspecting wife, 'I cheated on you and have a son to prove it.' Congratulations. You ask me what difference it makes; frankly, not much. Once a cheater, always a cheater. Once a liar, always a liar. You had two weeks to come clean after that phone call from *your son*." Betty laid great stress on the last two words. "You did not say a single word to me. Just because I was in the other room, did you think I was deaf? I was not asleep, I heard you. I have heard enough of this whole sordid story. I just wondered when and how you would tell me." She stood up and left Ed in the dark. Ed watched her figure in the dim kitchen light passing the counter. She did not stop as she picked up the jewelry box and disappeared from his sight.

When he decided to retire for the night, he found the bedroom door locked. Betty did not respond to his calling. He finally gave up begging her and settled down in the guest bedroom. The next morning he could not find her, she had already gone somewhere. *She may have gone to her sister,* he thought. *She must have hurried to tell her about last night. Always the sister, always the brother-in-law, never me,* Ed thought bitterly. *I was good enough to secure her a life of luxuries, anything she wanted, and not only what she needed. Yet, she kept me tagging along as an unnecessary appendage, or rather like a necessary, but unwanted one.*

Indeed, as soon as the first hint of sunrise manifested the breaking of a new day, Betty drove to her sister and brother-in-law. They both were still in bed when Betty arrived. Over breakfast, she poured out her all-consuming bitterness. Both listened to her salacious details sympathetically. They commiserated by recalling every nuance of Ed's misbehavior and repeated every vicious gossip they ever heard about him. After a lengthy discussion, they suggested her to tell everything to her children first, and then kick the cheating bastard out of the house.

9

It is wise to remember that you are one of those who can be fooled some of the times.

––––––––

Laurence J. Peter

One day, everyone noted a well-dressed, middle-aged man in a dark business suit, as he was escorted through the hospital. He was accompanied by Ed Jamison and his hatchet-woman secretary, Sarah. Shortly thereafter, he was seen in the rarely used conference room in deep discussion with Dr. Ramsey and Dr. Marshall, the head of surgery. Finally the entire medical staff met him during a special meeting called by Dr. Ramsey. It was then that he was introduced as Mr. W. Randolph Lawler, the new CEO. The change in leadership was dropped on the subordinates as an unexpected bomb: no one could predict that it was coming.

Ed Jamison appeared to be as jovial as always in his farewell speech, saying, "I thank everyone from the bottom of my heart for the support and labor you have always shown me. I could not have made a better decision in my life when I accepted the position here and started working with you. I can only ask you to continue the same toward Mr. Lawler." He only said his retirement was long overdue and now he was excitedly planning to do all the things he has always wanted to do, but never had time before.

The gossiping tongues soon began to whisper that Sarah reported his every move to the Board of Directors, who in return demanded his resignation on his return from Baltimore. Supposedly his failed attempt to secure a joint venture with the University Medical School and Hospital was the last nail in his coffin. Everyone suspected that the rest of the nails were delivered one by one through emails, text messages, and vicious insinuations by his secretary. They all had but one common source, Sarah. Apparently, Ed Jamison had to learn the hard way what even the ancient Greek philosophers knew: a scorned lover was a nightmare of an enemy.

Of course, these were only gossips spilled by the rumor-mills of the hospital. The topic became subject of much clandestine discussion, but only after each party made certain no uninvited person could overhear them. In the end, all remained rumors. No one knew the truth. After all, what are gossips but carefully revealed combinations of truths and half-truths?

After a brief confusion, the physicians' daily work continued uninterrupted. Their position was not influenced much by the coming and going of administrators. Essentially a change made in the higher echelon did not filter down to their level to make any difference in their way of attending the sick. Whether it was Jamison or Lawler on the top, they treated all the patients alike.

The Physician's Lounge was the perfect Petrie-dish to learn what was going on in the medical facility. Usually, the hospitalists kept complaining of being overwhelmed with unnecessary admissions, claiming Ferguson and his ER staff admitted every single person either for medical necessity or for fearing legal complications.

"Yeah, you go in with a hangnail, get a complete

body CT scan, and then we are called to admit." Dr. Pribus, one of the hospitalists, remarked sarcastically.

The subspecialists were almost all consultants, and they tried to remain equally charming with everyone because their referrals depended on the goodwill of the admitting doctor. Only the surgeons kept whining over every little alteration in their schedule. True, they did it while fully recognizing their own importance and casually mentioning their financial contribution to the hospital.

"What's going on, Dr. Ramsey? Did you kill someone lately?" Young Dr. Pribus turned to the head of ICU. "I have heard the patients drop in your department like flies."

"Well, we try, but they come in critically ill. Sometimes, regardless of what we do, they die in spite of all our efforts." Ramsey managed to smile between two bites of his food.

"If nothing else, they get excellent nursing care especially over certain weekends." Evidently, Dr. Siddiqui's oversight made the news among the staff. Before Dr. Ramsey could respond, Marsha Redcliff appeared in the doorway, shouting, "Everyone listen. I just came from the ER and gave tPA to a stroke patient. You have to hear this, it's incredible."

A dead silence prevailed in the room as they all turned towards her, expecting some miraculous resolution. Instead, she started with a "You won't believe it. I got a call for an acute stroke so I rushed to the ER. The woman is sitting on a stretcher, an upside-down newspaper in her hand; she is pretending to read it. Her husband is at the bedside. She talks gibberish. You can't understand a word that she says. So I turn to him to tell me what happened. I am in a hurry, I have like fifteen minutes left to give the tPA, and they almost ran out of time. Anyway, her husband tells me, 'She got up at six and read the paper first like every morning. Except it was upside down just like now. I thought it was smart. She tried to challenge her brain by reading it this way. When I complimented her, she answered me in total rubbish. I tried to talk with her discussing the articles in the paper but she did not make any sense. After a while I thought she might have a little problem so we came to the hospital.'

"All along, I continued questioning as I examined her. I soon discovered they lived twelve miles away, on the far side of the university. It has to be, they passed it on their way to our hospital. Naturally, my next inquiry was how come the ambulance didn't take them there? I thought I did not hear him correctly when he replied 'Oh, we didn't come by ambulance. We came on a tandem bike. You see, she likes to exercise and I thought this way she gets her morning workout.'"

The elemental burst of laughter was sprinkled with disbelief, "No one, not at our age, is that stupid!" and "Marsha, you made it up." The incredulity was almost palpable as they imagined the man driving the tandem bike while the stroking out woman pedaled behind him.

"Cross my heart and hope to die! This is why they almost ran out of time." Marsha laughed.

"C'mon, what were they, total idiots?"

"I guess they are just educated imbeciles. He is the Dean of the School of Chemistry."

"No. It's impossible. Are you kidding me?"

"Imagine, he is the role model, the teacher! Pity his students, not him. He deserves the Darwin Award."

"Wait, it's not over yet," Marsha interrupted the merriment, "When I took her up to ICU, he asked me, 'When can I bring in her elliptic machine? She would want to use it every day.' Can you believe it? In return, I asked him, 'Do you see a room in here for an exercise machine? This is not Planet Fitness but an intensive care room. Just go home and rest. You must be shaken up with what happened to your wife.' He left on his tandem bike. He bicycled home twelve miles just as they came here, on a two lane highway in the morning traffic. I have never seen anything like this." They all laughed while shaking their heads incredulously.

"Anything is possible," one of the hospitalists added to Marsha's story, "Once I had a woman with a frontal lobe hemorrhage. She was brought into the ER six hours later because her husband thought she was angry enough not to speak with him after they had a fight. When he finally found her half-dead on top of the bed, he realized she was not angry. She just had a bleed in her brain and could not talk."

"How about the one who refused to take warfarin anticoagulation because it was also used in a rat-killer, and he would not take 'rat poison'? So he rather died of multiple embolisms. Blows your mind, doesn't it?" The other hospitalist shook his head.

They all chimed in, recalling something unusual from the past. Once the quick lunch break was over, they returned to work one by one. Only a few remained in the dining room finishing their lunch. The kitchen staff got going by removing the leftovers and cleaned up the food line. If anyone missed the lunch, they only got cold sandwiches. The standard joke was "What does a latecomer get from Jeffrey Dahmer for dinner? A cold shoulder." Everyone tried to avoid the cold food after hearing the dark humor.

"Not to change the subject, but who do I report sexual harassment to?" Suddenly the room got quiet and they all stared at the statuesque, golden-blonde, young intern.

"Who dared to harass you? Let me teach him a lesson.

I will not tolerate anyone taking you from me. I will fight him!" Pribus mockingly rose to her defense.

"C'mon man, I was serious."

"I guess you have to talk to the Administration. Who was it?"

But the offended blonde just waved her hand and left the dining room. One of the older internists instantly complained, "I need to raise awareness of discrimination."

"What happened to you?" The shocked Pribus turned to him.

"I have never been harassed sexually. This is discrimination." The man replied, but his last words were drowned in laughter.

"Is there such a thing as male sexual harassment? I guess it could be though I never heard of any," the gastroenterologist remarked.

"Nah, men would call it a dream come true instead of harassment," chimed in a woman surgeon.

"Did you get that information from the 'Sturgeon General'?" They all found the new title funny.

Marsha quietly contemplated on what she heard. Interestingly no one ever harassed her sexually. She carried herself in a way that did not invite personal remarks. She remained friendly without fraternizing, respectful without being too close. The secret to be treated as a lady was to be a lady.

Then she remembered one incident. According to today's standards, it could have been a sexual harassment. It just never occurred to her. She considered the man coarse and lacking manners, that's all. Early in her carrier one of her instructors told her to walk down the hallway for something and called after her that he had seen better legs than hers though hers were OK. Marsha quickly retorted by yelling back at him, "See, this just proves how smart you were to hire me for my brain and not for the look of my legs." In the hearing distance, everyone started laughing and the man never made any further inappropriate remarks to her.

The few minutes of peace and lighthearted mood were wiped out by the sudden loudspeaker booming across the hospital, "Code Blue, second floor, room 234". Marsha left instantly, realizing the man in 234 was her new patient, Deante Jefferson. She raced to the second floor noting there were several nurses already crammed in his room. Two hospitalists arrived simultaneously, one yelling, "When you get to the point to 'call a physician', I am right behind you." The nurse stepped aside, and he took over. Marsha calmly watched from a distance as they instructed the dazed black man to look in this way then that, smile, lift an arm or a leg, and repeat some words. When they discovered the man was weak on his right side, one of them ordered a STAT CT of the brain, suspecting a stroke. They were sure of the diagnosis and needed no input from the neurologist standing in the doorway.

Marsha was certain it was not a stroke but something else. This "something" bothered her in the presentation, bothered her just enough to have a nagging doubt. It just didn't feel right; it did not look like a stroke. She decided not to leave, but keep an eye on the development. As she kept guard, the patient slowly changed, almost as if he were in a trance. He no longer carried out the instructions as before. Next, his eyes became glazed and slowly shifted to the left. Everything slowed down. Marsha had the sudden impression she was watching an old, silent movie in slow motion. The patient's eyes got stuck on the left and he did not look back again.

Now Marsha jumped forward and quickly ordered an injectable sedative. Both hospitalists stared at her, stunned to be speechless and only their puzzled expressions questioning her order. She calmly announced, "This is not a stroke. This is a seizure." Suddenly the still life shattered as the man started to jerk rhythmically. After two doses of Ativan, his seizure was aborted. As his limbs became limpid, he fell into a deep sleep. He did not even know when they transferred him to ICU.

Mr. Jefferson had four more seizures in ICU. He did not respond to the medications as Marsha expected. The blood work and CT of the brain were negative. None of the tests indicated a reason for seizing this much. Finally, she put him into a medically induced coma, hoping it would stop the abnormal brain activity.

At night, she looked up seizures in her old textbooks. She felt a heavy stone rolling off of her shoulders when she confirmed every step that she took was according to the neurology standards. Yet, she did not come up with a diagnosis. Seizures were just symptoms, one of the manifestations of an underlying cause. There had to be a reason which triggered them. What was the cause? She could not be satisfied with the idea that it was a functional disorder. She read her books until she fell asleep.

The next morning Mr. Jefferson's medications needed to be changed again, because in spite of being in a coma and completely motionless, his brain's electrical activity registered ongoing seizures. She ordered a continuous electroencephalogram and stopped between her patients frequently to check the monitor. Finally, the seizures stopped. Her next dilemma almost instantly cropped up. When was it time to revert his coma? Would he be back having seizures if she stopped his drugs? How could she guess it? What would be the best decision? What if the step she took was wrong? Every step also dragged along a potentially negative consequence. Marsha was back to the drawing board and back to her textbooks. When she found no answers, she put the heavy textbook down and started to think.

She talked to herself the same way as if she were a resident, and her favorite professor would be guiding her through a difficult case.

"So, the patient had intractable seizures. Never had one before, these were new-onset seizures. Something must have happened to cause them. What do you think happened to him? Think of the seizure triggers, Marsha." "Yes, I did. There were no head traumas or infectious disease symptoms. No sleep deprivation. No drug or alcohol abuse history. Toxicology was negative."

"Good thinking. How was his social life?"

"His life seemed stable with no recreational drug use history. Denied sexually transmitted diseases. As a matter of fact his family claimed he led an impeccable life. He was a moral man, a retired minister."

"That doesn't mean much. Perhaps, any unusual stress in the recent past? Something out of the ordinary? Was he consuming energy drinks or taking certain medications?"

"No, I don't think so. What stress would he have? That some members of his congregation sinned? Not likely. Nothing else jumped out of his history, either."

"How about a family history? Any seizures? Any abuse in his past?"

"None. He seemed to have a close-knit family. No one had similar symptoms or epilepsy."

Yet, something else was bothering her, something that she couldn't explain. Mr. Deante Jefferson was a very good looking, almost robust black man evidently keen on physical activities. His very concerned visitor Barbara asked permission to stay at his bedside from morning to night. She also bragged to Dr. Redcliff that she was working with Mr. Jefferson to write a book of Bible teachings. Contrary to the much-heralded brilliance, the manuscript was scribbled in pencil on pieces of scrap paper. The handwriting was childish, with frequent spelling and grammatical errors, and time and again illogical. Dr. Redcliff thought perhaps early dementia was the cause of these findings. Just one more piece of the puzzle, she thought.

This is when the lightning hit her. Maybe his wife could tell her something which could confirm her suspicion and lead to the dementia diagnosis. Mr. Jefferson's visitor was no stranger to her; Marsha talked with her every day. Barbara had many questions and needed thorough explanations for each minuscule change. She wanted to learn every detail of each test or drug. She seemed exceedingly concerned with his care, which in return cost Marsha hours. Barbara kept talking to her and even walked with her down the hallways just to continue her monologue. Only ducking in a patient's room saved Marsha from the relentless inquiries. While pursuing the elusive diagnosis, she decided to call the patient's wife to ask for specific details which may have occurred prior to the onset of his illness.

"Mrs. Jefferson, this is Dr. Redcliff from Cecilia Beach Hospital. You remember me: I am your husband's neurologist. Do you have a few minutes? I need some information."

"Who are you? Doctor who?" The voice was cold and unfamiliar.

"Dr. Redcliff. I talked to you earlier today at your husband's bedside."

"My husband is in Cecilia Beach? In a hospital? Why?"

"He had recurrent seizures. We call it status epilepticus. Don't you remember me? You had so many questions, Barbara, I could not forget you." Marsha chuckled, but was clearly perplexed.

"Excuse me," the obviously offended voice dragged

out the words, "The name is Elvira. Barbara is his live-in caregiver. You probably talked with her. She lives thirty miles away. I never was at your hospital or laid eyes on you. Now what do you want to 'aks' me?"

Marsha swallowed hard. "Thank you for clearing this up. Indeed, I had several long meetings with Mr. Jefferson's caregiver and assumed it was his wife."

Mrs. Jefferson frostily interrupted Marsha, "He is not a Mister, but a Reverend. Please address him properly."

Marsha did not want to make enemies, so she continued as if she were not corrected like a naughty three-year-old child. "I beg your pardon Mrs. Jefferson. Good thing you told me this. I appreciate your input. I called you because your husband had recurrent seizures and so far I couldn't find a good explanation why he developed them. Would you happen to know any reasons?"

"I thought that's why you 'was' being paid." Mrs. Jefferson flatly announced.

"Truly, this is what I do." Marsha swallowed hard then continued, "Perhaps it would be better to meet and talk in person. Would it be possible for you to come to the hospital tomorrow for a family conference? This way, everyone involved would be updated and kept on the same page. How about after lunch? I realize you live far away, but an after-lunch meeting would give you enough time not to be pressured."

"I guess I could get there to help you out." Mrs. Jefferson hung up the phone without saying a thank you or a good bye.

After staring incredulously at the dead phone for a long time, Marsha slammed it down so hard that a corner of the plastic receiver cracked. With her customary pleasantness gone, she uttered a few non-church words. Thank Heaven she lived alone, no one heard her outburst.

Next day the meeting unfolded the family secrets. Barbara was the good Reverend's mistress and they lived together on the beach. Elvira stayed in the marital property and refused to grant him a divorce, clinging to her married status. Both women begged Dr. Redcliff to do everything for this man. After all, he was irreplaceable, a brilliant Reverend, an upright and moral man, and a pillar of the community. Elvira Jefferson even grabbed Dr. Redcliff's hand and pressing it to her ample bosom stated, "Money *'ain't'* an object. If I *'has'* to, I *'sells'* one of *'them'* cars or the house. Nothing matters. Your job is to concentrate on his health. Don't you worry about your money; I'll personally *'pays'* you if the insurance *'don't'.*"

In two days, the diagnosis became clear. The righteous reverend, also known as the pillar of the community, had advanced neurosyphilis. Deante Jefferson was transferred to the University Hospital to the care of the combined Infectious Disease and Neurology Departments. His seizures stopped. The medication cocktail Dr. Redcliff created for him apparently controlled them.

"Whoa, Dr. Redcliff you asked for it and you got it, didn't you? Tell me, did you expect the diagnosis of syphilis?" Dr. Ramsey benevolently smiled at Marsha. "I bet it was a surprise."

"Well, it was. But that's why I am here; it's just part of my job. See I was right: I have always said there was a good reason to stay out of bed!" Marsha walked away.

Dr. Ramsey stopped in his tracks, hoping her last sentence had no hidden meaning. He started to turn away, wondering how much and what Dr. Redcliff may have known, and then he called after her, "Amazing. What's on your mind Dr. Redcliff?"

"If you knew what was on my mind, you could not print it."

"You know you are lucky you didn't live in the

middle-ages. You would be burnt at a stake just for being a female practicing medicine."

"Thanks. I thought you would say for being a witch. I am sure you wouldn't have added more wood to the fire, am I correct?" laughed Marsha and left him standing in the middle of ICU.

Two months later, Reverend Deante Jefferson's insurance rejected payment on the grounds of long-expired membership and failure to pay the monthly dues. The hospital wrote off the accrued expenses and refused to reimburse the consulting physicians. The neurology bills sent to Barbara were returned with "Addressee Unknown." The following week Dr. Redcliff received back Elvira's mail with a printed message on the envelope "Moved, no forward address." Neither woman ever answered the phone.

10

Heav'n has no Rage, like Love to Hatred turn'd,
Nor Hell a Fury, like a Woman scorn'd.

William Congreve

Only four patients were waiting to be called into the examination area by Dr. Ramsey's assistant. Two had portable oxygen tanks with clear plastic tubes hooked to the nose and one periodically gasped air through his open, bluish discolored lips. A well-dressed woman sat further away from the group and read an old magazine. She did not seem to be interested in the ongoing conversation, though she keenly listened to the wheezing and breathless remarks.

"Do you have to come for monthly visits, too?" A waxy skinned, older man inquired. The other responded with a "Yeah, he wants me here every month, but I don't know why. He doesn't do anything, just tells me to use my oxygen. Like I wouldn't. Sure."

"Same here. You didn't figure it, yet? He wants to get an office visit payment. That's what he does. All doctors are the same. Don't do anything and collect money." He suddenly stopped talking, then slowly got up and followed the nurse to the inner sanctuary.

The sad little office lacked colors as much as the

patients did. Everything was in a bland, faded shade of beige. Neither the walls, floors, nor the woodwork appeared to welcome the patients. The whole office conveyed the message of being functional without a shred of unnecessary pleasantness. The drab mood seemed to be contagious as if the employees were infected by it, too. Only Beth, Dr.'s Ramsey's ever cheerful nurse practitioner seemed to stick out from this sea of depressive, beige milieu. Even Beth thought of herself as the proverbial swan that had accidentally landed in the midst of a flock of ducks.

The young woman was actually quite attractive, but at her age all young women are pretty. Youth by itself is alluringly charming. Her face had a pleasant smile and her child-like, little girl's voice called for instant attention and raised the gallant protector in every man. Dr. Ramsey enjoyed her work and personality. In the beginning, he appreciated her looks and valued her work, but lately, he reveled in her congeniality more. Since he discovered her agreeable nature, he started to spend much more time in the office after the patients and staff had left. It was a perfect set-up he thought as his occasional overtime could not make anyone to suspect of any covert activity.

The only problem was that lately Beth became a bit clingy. She was still the same as before. Any time he wanted to be with her, she willingly stayed. She always assured him of her unending affections. Yet, in spite of her endless eagerness to please him, a slight uncomfortable feeling recurred as he reflected on the future. He could not shake the nagging thoughts off that somehow he got more than what he bargained for in the beginning. These were only rare fleeting thoughts, so he went ahead and enjoyed the affair without further idea about the future.

Then the sweet and comfortable set up unexpectedly shattered to pieces. Without warning, his wife appeared at his work and Dr. Ramsey suddenly had a come-to-Jesus encounter. After slamming the door, she steadily raised her voice at him.

"Sit down and don't you dare to interrupt me." Dr. Ramsey couldn't imagine what got into his wife. Friday was always the busiest day in the office; the schedule was full from anticipation for the two day weekend ahead; everybody called for a last minute medication refill. He had neither the time nor the mood to have a spousal instruction in his office; he usually had enough of it at home.

"I want this bimbo out of here, today. Now! I am not putting up with her. I will deal with you later. You're supposed to work and not screw around with your staff."

"Honey, calm down," started Dr. Ramsey, to no avail. His pacifying soft tone was drowned out in her rapidly fired accusations. He was an already convicted criminal in the process to be justly executed. All of his wife's demons were lined up in a firing squad aiming at him, ready to fire.

"Don't you honey me as long as this... this... What should I call her? Whore? OK, I'll be nice. As long as your mistress is here. Or mattress. Whichever you prefer."

"Oh my God, lower your voice! You are in a medical office filled with people! What do you want?"

"I want her out of here. Now. Unless you fire her today, Monday morning I am in the divorce attorney's office and I swear I will drag you through hell. I will take your two boys, your house, and your business, everything you ever owned. By the time I am done with you, I guarantee you, you will have nothing. Absolutely nothing. You will be finished in Cecilia Beach too, I promise you. You couldn't hide from me. Wherever you go, I will be there to ruin you. I swear I will."

She stood in front of his desk, her two clenched fists

planted with iron determination on the edge. Ramsey knew his hot-blooded Italian wife enough to realize she was ready to punch him at any moment.

"OK, OK. I will let her go. Just lower your voice, please."

"Now. Call her in the office now and do it," his wife demanded as she turned towards the door, "Or do you want me to call her?"

"No, no, no, don't do it. I will. Just please be quiet while I talk to her." Dr. Ramsey had no choice, but to do what this insane woman dictated. Unless, of course, he wanted to lose his family, reputation, home, and business. The alternative was much worse than getting rid of his assistant.

"Beth, please come to my office". He talked into the intercom, although by now, everyone already heard his wife's voice.

The nurse entered, her face paler than usual, but her voice steady. "You don't have to tell me anything, I already heard it, and so did everyone else including the patients and probably the next door people, too. I will not work in such an unprofessional place any more. I am a licensed professional and I demand respect. I quit as of now." She faced Mrs. Ramsey and with a hint of arrogance, she hissed, "Enjoy what you got. A real class-act!" She left before either of them could respond.

Dr. Ramsey literally had to hold his wife down to prevent further escalation of the matters and creating more scenes. All of his talent of diplomacy and soothing were needed until he finally managed to cajole and sweet-talk his wife to the back door. She slammed the door of her Mercedes while promising him to continue the subject at home. He consciously registered if he wanted to save whatever was left of his existence; he had to agree with all of his wife's iron-clad terms.

In the interim, Beth Young arrived to her boyfriend's

condo. After leaving Ramsey's office she headed straight to him. She wanted to be the first to tell him the news of her quitting, otherwise, who knows what the gossip would carry to him. When she entered, Adam was getting ready for work. To his surprised inquiries, she told him in details the dire circumstances which forced her to quit the job she liked so much.

"You know Babe, I couldn't take it anymore. That office was like a wasp-nest: the girls were insanely jealous of me and crossed me every day, as often as they dared. I could not help it. It was not my fault that they were only trained for office help, and I had a diploma. It was just getting to be too much, too crazy. Way too much."

"So why did not Dr. Ramsey set them straight?"

"I don't know. I guess, he didn't dare to say anything to them." Beth looked real upset and ready to cry. "Today was especially bad. Imagine this, one woman went into his office and complained about me. We all could hear it through the closed door, because she raised her voice. Can you believe it, she dared to call me names. I think she might have referred to you, because she said I would lay with anyone. I was really offended, because you are not just an 'anyone'. After hearing this insult, I marched right in and quit on the spot. I had no choice. How could I work at a place where I couldn't get any respect? Neither from my boss nor from the girls? Nobody would carry out my orders anymore. They just completely sabotaged me. I had no choice but to quit," she repeated it.

"First of all, they shouldn't put their nose in our business. What you do in your private life doesn't concern anyone else but you and me. Second, is the office staffed with innocent virgins? Hardly. They have no right to feel superior to anyone else. They are not the moral police. Third, your dear Dr. Ramsey was a wuss if he didn't dare to speak up. Was he afraid? Of what? Do they have anything on him? They had to know something really bad to be able to control him." He stopped shaving and stared at her with half of his face still covered by the shaving foam.

"By golly, I think you are right. They must be blackmailing him if they have such power over him and can manipulate him left and right." Beth smiled at him through her tears. "I always said you know people like no one else. I told you, you were smart. Ah, you know everything!" Her little girl's lips could not stop trembling.

"OK. So you quit. Good for you. Maybe this way you prevented more problems than you know. What if he put a move on you? No, you don't need that kind of headache. I know these doctors, trust me. I see what they do in the hospital." He stepped to her and hugged her. "With me, you are always safe; this is your home, too. Forget about them. Next week you could look for another job. You have good qualifications. You'll get any job you want. How about if I ask my boss? Our ER always hires nurse practitioners. Hey, we could work together. You at daytime, I am at night. Two RNs would be like running our private practice. What do you say love?" He gently wiped the tears off of her face.

"No, don't call anyone, not yet. I want to get a job on my own. I don't want you to ever feel I didn't pull my own weight here or that you had to support me. It's enough that I have to rely on you until I get something." Beth seemed to disappear in his bear hug.

"Of course, nothing to it. Maybe in another year we can save enough dough to get married. You still want to be married to me, I hope. You did not change your mind, did you?"

"C'mon, don't even joke about that. Quitting that lousy place has nothing to do with us."

"All right, soon-to-be Mrs. Whittaker. Now let me get going or we both will be out of jobs. How can I get a nice rock on your finger then? Don't tempt me. We don't have that much time now, but be ready when I get home."

After Adam Whittaker, RN left his home Beth sighed in relief. Adam would take care of everything. She was at home with him. All would be so perfect if only he had an MD after his name and not an RN. On the other hand he was not at home most of the time. He worked five nights in a row and slept most of the day. She could manage that.

11

Every child comes with the message that
God is not yet discouraged of man.

———

Rabindranath Tagore

Marsha Redcliff had a busy morning. During the night, the ER admitted quite a few patients, and ever since she stepped in the hospital, they called for her to do non-stop consultations. If that were not enough, she got a call from the technician. He said there was a stack of EEG waiting for her to be interpreted.

"How many did you say?" Marsha searched her mind for how many EEGs she ordered. No matter how she counted, there were four extra tests.

"Nine, there are nine now. I just finished the last one on Mrs. Dohlmeyer. It looks OK, though." The EEG tech was good so Marsha knew he would have notified her immediately if he saw any abnormalities. He was also the technician who called her when Reverend Jefferson had the epileptic fits. After working on that man day and night, Marsha learned to trust the technician's judgments. She also liked and respected him since she overheard him talking compassionately to the patients.

"Who ordered the EEG? I did not even know this patient. I have no such name on my list."

"Dr. Pribus, the hospitalist, ordered it," replied the technician.

"Pribus? Without even calling me? If he knows as much as a neurologist, then he does not need me. Let him interpret it." Marsha hung up the phone.

Just in case she browsed Mrs. Dohlmeyer's record. After all Pribus might have found some indication for an EEG, she thought. The Devil never sleeps. The further she read the angrier she got. Apparently, Mrs. Dohlmeyer was the wife of a well to do businessman who frequented her general practitioner. Her husband happened to be on the Board of Directors in Cecilia Beach Hospital. This week however, Mrs. Dohlmeyer was advised that her doctor was on vacation and she should go to the ER with her problems. She did. All she complained about was a single solitary nightmare. No headache, no dizziness, no loss of conscience, and especially no seizures.

After a completely normal head CT, her husband insisted on her admission to the hospital. "In order to avoid some legal consequences, just might you want to discover the cause for this disturbing development, don't you?" He poignantly questioned the overwhelmed ER physician.

In the interim Mrs. Dohlmeyer calmly enjoyed the action swirling around her. Marsha decided Dr. Pribus probably wanted only to appease the husband by ordering an EEG. There was really no other indication for doing it. Ok, then let him interpret it, decided Marsha. She didn't worry about it further for she knew sooner or later Dr. Pribus will ask for her help. What was the definition of a double- blind study? Two orthopods looking at an EEG. Or, in this case, a hospitalist.

She stormed down the hallway, fighting her way through several family members who camped out in front of a room. She knew the patient there. It was a young gypsy boy with long history of epilepsy. His parents mobilized the entire clan and sat vigil in the foyer. When they brought in a hotplate and started to cook their meal in the corridor, the security guard stepped in and tried to escort them out. This resulted in loud wailing interspersed with earsplitting cursing. As soon as they claimed they were singled out for no other reason but being gypsy, the administrator allowed them to stay. In exchange, from then on, they cooked the meals in the parking lot.

A few rooms away, Marsha quietly approached the young woman who turned to the wall. She was motionless though awake. Her huge dark eyes sunk deep in their sockets surrounded by dusky skin folds. Her temples caved in and her teeth looked abnormally large in the emaciated face.

"How do you feel today, Mrs. Baylor? Has the back pain eased with the new medication? Is there anything I could do for you?" Marsha asked her softly.

She got no response. She probed again, "Did you see your baby yesterday? She is getting big, and she is so beautiful. I think she will look just like you when she grows up."

"I will not see that," whispered Mrs. Baylor.

"I realize you may not," began Marsha slowly, "But it's important to know she will carry on your genes, your legacy. She will be your continuation."

"My continuation, you say 'my continuation.' Do you realize what it means to me?" Mrs. Baylor turned to Marsha. "It means I will not be here. I will not take her to school, not see her graduate, and I won't dress her on her wedding day. I will be gone. She will grow up without ever knowing me. She will have no mother."

She wiped off her tears and continued with exasperation, "How will she ever know there was a woman who wanted her more than anything in this whole wide world? Who planned every day of her pregnancy with loving thoughts about how to make her child's life the best? How? You tell me." Mrs. Baylor's burning glance searched the doctor's face.

"Mrs. Baylor, your husband will tell her everything about you." Marsha gently stroked the dying woman's thinned out hair.

"Really? You haven't heard he asked for a divorce? Everyone else did." Marsha was speechless. She did not hear a word about Mr. Baylor's last visit.

"Let me tell you what's going on," Mrs. Baylor began as anger and sadness choked her voice, "I delivered my little girl six months ago. I did not stop bleeding so they did a little procedure to clean my uterus from some tissue stuck there after the birth. That tissue was cancer. Choroid carcinoma; an aggressive, nasty killer. Yesterday my husband visited me here and told me I could never be the wife or the mother he needed, so he better get rid of me and find someone to replace me. A substitute, and I did not even die yet! And you tell me he would teach my little girl about me?"

Marsha was speechless. Animals did not do that to their mate. She just stood by the bedside holding Mrs. Baylor's skin and bony hand and feverishly searched her mind to say something; something which eases the anguish of a departing soul. But what was there to say?

"Mrs. Baylor I don't know what to say or do for you. But I promise you, whatever medically is possible, I will do. The ER paged me; I'll have to go there. I will come back later if it's OK with you. In the meantime, shall I send in the Chaplain? He is a nice man, he would listen to you. You would like him, I am sure. And whatever you say stays here in this room. How about a visit with him, what do you think?" She called the Chaplain then headed to the ER.

The ER bay was dark, only the night lights giving a little

visibility. She asked the necessary questions, examined the patient, and ordered an infusion for the migraine headache. Half an hour later, she was called back for the patient developed intractable vomiting. The nurse impersonally accounted for the prior events, "She got the DHE you ordered and I gave her the antiemetic ten minutes later."

"Say that again," Marsha asked, and "Which one did you give first?" Although she realized the ordered sequence was reversed, she wanted the nurse to admit she made a mistake.

"The DHE. She had a terrible headache." The nurse felt justified for changing the order from antiemetic first and the anti-migraine medication second.

"Then don't be surprised when she starts throwing up. The DHE caused it. The side effect is severe vomiting. Why else would I explicitly order the arrangement I want the drugs to be given?"

Marsha was annoyed. "Fill out a 'Medication Error' form and next time, please follow directions the way they are written. There is a reason for it other than spending my time here with a relatively passable penmanship." Dr. Ferguson already medicated the patient for the nausea, and she stopped her retching.

Just then, the ICU called her for an urgent evaluation. Josè relayed the message of a three year-old little girl in brain death. Marsha flatly announced, "I am not a pediatric neurologist. I will not see her."

"Uh, Dr. Redcliff don't do this to me. Do me a favor, please see her. Dr. Pacheco is away, we have no other neurologist available. Hey, you can do no wrong, she is already brain dead." Josè convincingly continued the persuasion.

The little girl looked like a porcelain doll. Her straw blonde hair was arranged in a thick pleated ponytail.

Evidently, the nurses took special time to make her look her best, dressing and combing her hair as if she were a toy. Her huge blue eyes stared without recognition. Even before she started to examine her Marsha instantly noted there was no life in them.

She saw a few little bruises on her knees and forearm which might have only indicated an active child. In view of the obvious brain defect, Marsha harbored an uneasy feeling and doubted an innocent past.

"What happened to her?" She asked the RN standing on the opposite side of the bed, calmly watching the doctor flashing her light into the child's eyes.

"She fell off the sofa and landed on her head. The parents brought her to the ER."

"You're kidding me. This is not the result of a fall." They watched the child stiffening more with each touch, finally arching her back in an unnatural curve. She continued the contrived bending until her heels almost touched the back of her head. All along, her face had no change of expression, and her eyes remained vacant. Only her forehead shined with new beads of perspiration.

Damn Pacheco, just when she is needed she is nowhere to be found, thought Marsha. She already diagnosed the child but now she needed to find ways to confirm it.

"Do we have an ophthalmologist on call or is he missing in action, too?" She questioned the nurse.

"We have one, I think I saw Dr. Bell downstairs. He is the eye doctor I believe, correct? He might be still in house. Do you want me to call him or just wait until he shows up here? Although I don't believe we have any patients for him."

"Yes please, call him now." Marsha watched the nurse and wondered where he got his license. Probably bought it on eBay, she thought. He must have been recently hired because she has never seen him before. After finishing the evaluation, she asked Josè about the new nurse. She went directly to the source: Josè always knew everything.

"Chuck? He is Chuck Potts. He is new and is being oriented to the job this week. Don't need to bother with him, he is assigned to night shift, you won't see him much." As usual, Josè was a wealth of knowledge.

Leaving the ICU Marsha passed the family waiting room. A young woman dressed in dubious clean jeans and a stretched out polo was squeezing pimples on her chin. She propped a small mirror against the vase of some colorful silk flowers. Next to her, a young punk rested his legs on the table and snored with open mouth. Although she was never told, Marsha immediately thought of poor little Evie. She laid brain dead in ICU and these must be her parents. Well, at least they brought her to the ER, she ended her pondering.

She finished reviewing the last EEG when her phone rang. She answered with her official voice and usual response, "Dr. Redcliff. What can I do for you?"

"Nothing, you already did Marsha. It's Paul Bell. I saw your little girl, Evie Hill. Your suspicions were right, she has retinal hemorrhage. Actually, her eyes are full of blood. That kid was shaken to death. To brain death. There is nothing I can do for her. I don't believe you can, either. Sorry. Pretty little thing, what a shame! Whoever did it should be hung!"

Marsha liked good ole' Paul Bell, who never missed a diagnosis so he must have been correct this time, too. She really wished he would have been wrong. Beautiful Evie Hill was abused and irreversibly injured. She muttered half aloud, "Pacheco, Pacheco, you sure know when to have a day off! Now I have to face the police."

She circled back to the ER to get details of the admission of the three-year- old. Seeing no scalp trauma to indicate a fall, the ER doctor suspected child abuse.

He contacted the police as soon as he saw Evie's X-ray showed a couple of healed rib fractures. He added, "She arrived in a hypothermic state, her body felt cold, and her temp was way below normal. I don't know what they did to her. Either they did not bring her to the ER in time or they tied her to the hood of the car and drove her in."

Interesting detail but a morbid thought, Marsha concluded. She made a mental note to make sure the police knew it. Before the day was over, the police limited visits to Evie's bed. Her mother could see her only while being supervised and the mother's boyfriend was taken into custody. No matter how he yelled about knowing his rights and being falsely accused, the disgusted hospital staff agreed with the law: he had no place near Evie and certainly no place being seen by any of the nurses.

Marsha felt sad and emotionally drained. For a fleeting second, it even occurred to her to adopt the unfortunate little girl, although she realized how impossible an idea this was. Poor little Evie's parents did not deserve her. Her ignorant mother trusted her to a new boyfriend while she was away. She left her child with a felon, a felon who had a past with a criminal list as long as a Christmas wish list.

At the end Evie Hill was unfortunate to survive the shaken-baby trauma. If she died she would have been luckier. This way she would live, live without a single normal thought in her oxygen-deprived and damaged brain, her mind gone forever. Yet her healthy little body would survive the breathing machine, the tube feedings through the wall of her belly, the diapering and total caring she needed until some infection would claim her and end her earthly tortures.

Who would do all these things for her, who would care for her? Her uneducated, unsophisticated mother? She already delegated her responsibility to a criminal when Evie was a healthy three-year-old. Would she rise to the occasion now as her invalid child represented only unending chores? Hardly. The boyfriend faced criminal charges. Ten to one he would end up in jail for a couple of years and get out early only to be further educated in crimes by his cellmates.

In spite of her eternal optimism, Marsha Redcliff agreed with the ER doc: "Life sucked and at times even more."

12

On her way back to the inpatient rooms, Marsha felt as if she were a bag of popcorn. Just like popcorn jumping in every direction she was also in constant motion, pulled in many directions, yet, she had to look calm. It was lunchtime so she sharply detoured to the Doctor's Lounge. Maybe she wouldn't get paged for a few minutes while she grabbed a quick bite. She was surprised to see one of her colleagues with a good-sized shiner. With genuine concern, she inquired, "Oh my, whatever happened to you? Was it a car accident? I bet it must have hurt like hell."

The doctor avoided looking at her as he mumbled, "Yes, it was an accident, alright." He did not say anything more.

She jokingly continued, "Better than if someone punched you out, don't you agree?" He sharply looked up and stared at her but did not respond. Instead, he grabbed his food and left.

Marsha was confused. She felt embarrassed, mentally scolding herself for joking with the man. It occurred to her, perhaps, he did not have a sense of humor and took her seriously. She only knew him from the hospital, but they never talked, short of saying some niceties as they passed each other in the hallway. They shared a few patients, greeted each other, and silently suffered through the mandatory meetings. She recalled their first encounter after a particularly boring video presentation, "Too bad they turned on the light so soon. It was nice sleeping with you."

She sat down in a daze next to one of the hospitalists, but before she could have her first bite the hospitalist laughingly turned to her, "Leave it to you Dr. Redcliff, you tell them as it is, don't you? Now I know why the nurses call you Dr. Spicy!"

"What are you talking about?" Marsha stared at the young doctor in astonishment.

"Dr. Spicy is the nickname they call you. Haven't you heard it before? A minute ago, you just proved to me you fit that name perfectly. You told Dr. Reynolds exactly what he tried to hide, his black eye." He started to laugh and a couple of the other diners also chuckled.

"I don't get it," said Marsha, "how could he hide that black eye? There is no way anyone could miss it. Besides, if it was a motor vehicle accident why would he hide it? Was it his fault?"

"Motor vehicle accident, my foot. Although you might call it an accident." Now the nearby doctors were also smirking and started to chime in, all talking to Marsha. She looked from one to another still not comprehending what was going on.

"Honestly, you did not hear it? Two nights ago he was punched out by his lover's fiancé."

"Oh, my God! And I told him..." Marsha could not finish it. "I truly felt sorry for him and didn't mean anything by it. So help me I had no idea!"

About six months later one of her friends, an ICU nurse, privately gave her the lo-down. "You know, Dr. Reynolds had an ongoing affair with a nurse practitioner. Unbeknownst to him she also had another lover, a psychiatrist from the University Hospital. I don't know why but she seemed to specialize in physicians. Maybe she wanted to catch one for a husband," the nurse chuckled and then continued seriously.

"Unfortunately, Dr. Reynolds made a mistake and showed up on the wrong night at her place. Can you imagine that? He had a key so he simply entered the place hoping to surprise her. He carried a box of chocolate and some flowers to her to sweeten the unscheduled get together. To his greatest shock, he found his heart's desire in bed with the psychiatrist. The two men got into a shouting match which quickly turned to physical. When the psychiatrist knocked the box of chocolate to the floor, Reynolds pushed him away. He bumped into a chair, fell over it and landed hitting the wall. They started to bash each other. At the end the psychiatrist punched out Dr. Reynolds. How do you like that?"

Marsha was dumbfounded. She heard similar stories before but thinking of Dr. Reynolds the allergist and Dr. Stern the psychiatrist she could not picture either as any woman's burning desire. Reynolds badly needed a hip replacement, judging by his limp. He never appeared to be particularly well groomed, either. The psychiatrist sported a jet-black Afro and was fat. The general consensus was that "It was easier to jump over him than go around him." Both men were married and in their late fifties.

"No, it's impossible." Marsha was incredulous.

"Wait, that's not everything, there is more. Here comes the real juicy stuff. While the two were making the entire racket yelling at each other, the woman was screaming at them to stop. They just carried on as if they never heard her, smashing into furniture, and banging into the walls. The frightened neighbors called 911 hearing the ruckus. They thought the man next door was beating up his wife. They believed it was an ugly case of domestic abuse. Soon enough two policemen arrived. Their questioning revealed that neither of the two men were the owner of the condo. The woman said the owner was her fiancé and he was at work.

"One of the policeman decided, 'Ok, I'll call him' and he dialed his work. The fiancé left immediately for home to verify that the woman was legally staying there and it was with his permission. First he defended her 'She is my fiancée, of course she can stay in my house. Can't you see she is pregnant?' he asked. Both of the scantily dressed doctors were ready to collapse hearing the word 'pregnant'.

"Then he continued, 'I told her no problem, we were planning to get married anyway, we'll just do it a bit sooner. Honey, are you OK?' He turned to her with concern. Then he questioned the policemen, 'Did you charge and arrest the two burglars yet?'

"The two policemen looked at each other before responding him, 'Well, they are not exactly burglars.' Then they explained everything to him. The news took the wind out of his sail for sure. At the end the two men were let go with a citation for disturbing peace and domestic violence and the fiancé kicked the pregnant girlfriend out."

"Whatever happened to the baby? Whose was it?" Marsha inquired.

"Well, that's the funny part. As soon as the baby was born, the fiancé demanded a paternity test. The little girl was not his daughter."

"Was she Reynold's?" Marsha wondered.

"No, Stern was the father. Reynolds got off the easiest. All he paid for this fun was a black eye. Better than being the father, don't you think?"

"Stern? I can't believe it. He is so ridiculous. That jet-black, dyed Afro is outrageous." Masha could not shake off the mental image of the man.

"And that's when he is all dressed up. Imagine him naked!" The nurse doubled up with laughter.

"Don't even go there, now I will never be able to look at him without thinking of this! So, is he the father?"

"Yep, he is the daddy! No matter how Mommy Dearest demanded Dr. Stern to get a divorce, he stayed married to his wife. I have heard later the girlfriend wanted to catch a doctor and that's why she did it. I think all Stern did was get a job for her and now he pays child support to Beth."

"Beth?" Marsha looked up.

"Yes, Beth Young, the nurse practitioner. Don't tell me you didn't know it? Where do you live, you never hear anything? Of course, her ex-fiancé Adam Whittaker, an RN from the University Hospital ER, no longer talks to her. I'll bet he is thankful to discover what went on behind his back. He discovered it in the nick of time, too."

Marsha shook her head in disbelief, "Beth Young? Didn't they gossip about her and Dr. Ramsey before?"

"Same song, second verse. Or third. Come to think of it, it's actually the fourth." Her nurse friend laughed. "The only difference was then she had Ramsey, Adam, and the two other doctors alternating. Lately, she only had the three. She must have had stamina out of this world! I guess she earned her title of 'Iron Horse'."

She shook her head in amazement before she continued with a giggle, "Don't you ever wonder how come some women get men and others don't? They have all the fun. Must be nice to have a good relationship,

I should try it one day. But I am married. Anyway, I bet it was hard to keep the schedule going."

"I would say so, as the end result indicated. Don't envy her, this is not a relationship you would want."

"I was just kidding, I hope you know," her friend assured her, "Besides, I am an old married woman and if I wanted a relationship, I would look for one at home."

Marsha thought how lucky Dr. Ramsey was to cave in to his wife's demands. At the end everyone breathed at ease: Ramsey, Reynolds, and Adam, too. Dr. Stern only could blame himself.

Much later both Marsha and her nurse friend heard about the psychiatrist's greatest regret. Years before Dr. Stern put all his finances in his wife's name to avoid paying taxes. Now he owned practically nothing on his own and even half of that nothing had to be sent to support his new daughter.

13

It is the loose ends with which men hang themselves.

———

Zelda Fitzgerald

Ed Jamison didn't have much more than a lot of time on his hand. A year prior, he had a solid, stable family, a nice home in the suburbs, a big job which paid an almost seven figure salary, and a respectable position in his church and community. He had everything, including a dark secret. Once he exposed his secret, he lost it all.

After the revealing discussion of fathering a son, his wife demanded marriage counseling. She found an elderly, never married spinster who supposedly had all the qualifications to restore their marriage. Ed wondered how on Earth any counselor could advise on a subject she never experienced but he did not think it was wise to voice his doubts aloud. He dutifully showed up to the sessions and jumped through the flaming hoops his wife held in front of him.

After the first session, it was clear Ed was doomed. The counselor referred to him repeatedly as a "rapist" and recommended him to move out of the house "Until the wronged party settles everything in her mind and decides on the best method to reach a solution."

Ed stuffed his hatchback with his clothes and beddings and moved in the vacant summer home of his old friend. He ate his three meals in restaurants and attended every event in the greater Cecilia Beach vicinity. One day he ran into Dr. Redcliff. The area authors organized a book fair and to his greatest surprise, he found Marsha Redcliff behind a stack of books.

"That's a real surprise. I didn't know you are a published author of a book," Ed Jamison genuinely seemed to be flabbergasted.

"Excuse me, but as you can see, I have published three books, not one." Marsha proudly pointed at her table.

After Ed purchased a copy of each, he invited Marsha to dinner. The small German restaurant on the waterfront sparkled in the golden sunset. At a corner table an older woman talked quietly with a young man. She was elegantly dressed and her make-up, jewelry, and cloths indicated she had wealth. Marsha thought she must have been beautiful before the damage of time spoiled her looks. Now, she appeared like a once proud castle slipping away in the ruin of time.

Yet, Marsha had a twinge of envy looking at the attentive young man and the well-preserved lady. It was nice to see a mother and son having a quiet dinner. They reminded her of her family. Unfortunately, Marsha's children lived far and she could only spend a few days visiting them each year. She hoped this mother realized how fortunate she was to have such a nice son. A son who would rather dine with his mother than hang loose with his friends. He seemed to cater to her, paying special attention to all her needs. Shortly after Ed and Marsha were seated, the woman turned back and glanced at them. She called for the waiter, paid for their dinner, and they left. The young man politely helped her into her sparkling, black Maserati.

"Look at that car," Marsha turned to Ed, "Isn't it gorgeous? One day before I die, I want to have one. Of course, I better win the lottery before. Some people seem to have everything," she claimed with longing.

"Oh yes," Ed replied, "everything, including a young and handsome gigolo. I know this woman from my Country Club. Every year she has a different, good looking, young man to escort her. This must be her most recent lover, because I haven't seen him before." Marsha sat as if she was doused with cold water. So much for the image of a charming family picture.

Ed could not decide which was better, the gorgeous view or the mouthwatering meal. Marsha agreed the sauerbraten was delicious but, thought her spätzle was lighter. Then she immediately corrected herself, "I meant it used to be when I still cooked. I don't do much cooking since my kids left the house. It's not fun to do it for one person."

This seemed to open Ed's floodgate. "At least your children call you. Mine don't even talk to me since I had to move out. That is, the youngest still does somewhat. But my daughter wants nothing to do with me."

"Did you tell them what happened? Maybe if they would hear it from you ..."

Ed interrupted her, "There is nothing I could say or do to change their opinion. My wife already talked with them and poisoned their minds against me. Yet I still hope she will calm down. I do everything she tells me, maintain the house, got to clean the pool when the maintenance man was away, even delivered her groceries and so on. But so far she did not change her mind. Not yet, anyway. I want her to see that I would do anything to restore my family. Really I would, just to have them back. I hope if I comply with everything without any questions or objections she would calm down. I think I am on the right track, because last time she only called me a "bastard" without any expletive adjectives attached to it like before."

Marsha incredulously stared at the man. "Do you believe this is a good indication of her forgiveness? Or a base to restart a marriage? She is done with you. Can't you see it? Ed, what you don't know of women could fill a book!"

"Now why would you think so?" Ed wondered, clearly doubting whatever he was told.

"No, I don't think so, I know so. Don't forget I ran a family counseling center before I took this job in the hospital. I have heard it all before. I know what I'm talking about, trust me. Once you get through reading my books of Dating Games and the Land of Cotton, you will also see the light."

"But you are a neurologist, how could you?" Obviously, Ed was not convinced.

"C'mon, Dr. Jamison, I am board certified in both psychiatry and neurology. When a woman is done with a man and she has made a decision, trust me, nothing changes her mind. The more you cave in the least she respects you. She only makes the various demands on you to humiliate you further. Don't you see you are only a marionette and she pulls the strings? Have you seen anyone falling in love with a puppet? Except maybe Geppetto with Pinocchio. The way I gathered, she already decided you were Pinocchio, anyway. Frankly, you have to face it, she would be better off without you."

"How could you say that? You never even met her!" He sounded aggrieved.

"That's true, I haven't. Nevertheless, I know her thinking. It's so logical and so clear. Why should she put up with you and your philandering? Tell me. If she divorces you she gets half of everything. And, she has no further headache. Can't you see? With a divorce she can only improve her situation."

"That's probably true, because she would end up with half of everything which is a bit over a million and a half," Ed agreed, visibly proud of his achievement.

"Think of it Ed. She would get a million and a half. Don't forget she would get the house and all the furnishing. She remained in it and you left it. Have you heard of ownership? *'Who's in: will win; who doesn't stay: will pay.'* Correct? Plus she has the car. She still would have her family around her. You said she always was close to her sister. Well, the sister will replace you at every social function. You won't be missed. The kids will support mommy. You won't be needed. Nothing would change, only you would not be in the picture any more. Give me a single reason why she would need you?"

"Wow," Ed's voice came as if from a distance, "the way you put it, it is possible." He sat quietly for a long time. Marsha let him digest what was said. Suddenly he shook his head and with newly found conviction announced, "No, no, it's impossible. She wouldn't do that. Not for what I did four decades ago."

"Ed you better get it to your head. She is not going to divorce you over one single event. The way I see it, your marriage was existing only by habit. Be honest, isn't it true? The illegitimate son who made no demands on your wife was only the last drop to overflow her cup. She has already done her own things and probably was mentally prepared to live her life without you. If she had no other problems with you, do you think she would divorce you over a forty-year old one-night affair? You had to do much more than this to push her to the verge of divorce."

They sat silently for a while. Ed mulled over in his mind what he heard and decided that Marsha was probably wrong. He could eat crow, crawl in dirt, and beg his wife as long as it took, but he would be back the same as before. No, he did not want to start a new life at the same time when his job retired him. One major change was enough.

Marsha sat on the opposite end of the table, silently chastising herself for speaking her mind. If Ed was blind enough to continue the downhill slide what difference did it make to her? Yet...he would be soon divorced, he is intelligent, and still carries himself with dignity in spite of his history. She eyed him for a second then looked away. *Why bother,* she thought. *I am myself and I like me for who I am. I don't need a husband. I am not looking for a man to save me; I am able to save myself. I am not going to play the role of a stupid blonde, flutter my eyelids, and look up to him as if he were my savior just to catch him. Besides, for the first time in my life I feel confident and comfortable in my own skin. I don't want extra trouble. I've been there, done that.*

She finally broke the stillness, "Shall we go? Dinner was yummy, but I have a hard day tomorrow."

Ed replied, "Sure, thanks for sharing the evening with me. You know you are a very intelligent woman. I enjoyed talking with you. I am planning to go away to upper New York to stay at our summer home. We have a house on a lake near the Iroquois National Wildlife Reservation. It's absolutely breathtaking there. Of course I would stay only until I can return to home again. If I would send you an airplane ticket would you visit me one weekend? The house is of good size, has four rooms, you would be a guest. No obligations, just a visit. Have you seen the Niagara Falls? It's a couple of hours away, we could drive there."

"Hmm. No, I have never seen it, but always wanted to

take a glimpse. Perhaps, we'll see. Thanks for the invitation and thanks for dinner, too. We'll talk again."

Ed sent her a few text messages and pictures of his summer house and emails accounting all the repairs and additions he completed just to please his wife. Slowly the contacts became more and more infrequent before they stopped all together. A year later, clear out of the blue, he called her to meet him for breakfast. His divorce was about to be finalized just as she predicted. She declined Ed's invitation, claiming she had an early start; her first patient was scheduled at eight. She did not tell him in words, but essentially stated it clearly: if she wasn't his priority, she didn't want to be his option. She wanted to be more than just a back-up plan or a last resort.

Ed Jamison unperturbed continued his way to the West Coast without stopping by to say Good Bye. Soon he met a divorcee and four months later he got re-married and settled with his new wife near San Francisco.

14

*I have always held firmly to the thought that each one of us
can do a little to bring some portion of misery to an end.*

—————

Albert Schweitzer

It was a gorgeous sunny February day when Marsha Redcliff returned for her yearly follow up to Dr. Ramsey. It happened to be her birthday and she felt good. The previous year flew by fast with lots of work then she treated herself by taking her sons and their families to celebrate Christmas with her in the Bahamas. On her return, she tried to catch up with work and paying her bills.

When Dr. Ramsey's receptionist postponed her appointment by a month, she had no objections. After all, there were no new symptoms only her chronic cough and no one in Dr. Ramsey's office seemed to be concerned. The last two visits gave her the impression her care was more due to professional courtesy than due to a medical necessity. Regardless, at least Dr. Ramsey sympathized with her predicament because he prescribed all sort of inhalers, nebulizers, and chest compression vest to ease her cough. Too bad neither had worked.

As she watched the dust particles dance in a beam of light while waiting in the sad little room for the doctor, she started to cough. It was one of her relentless ongoing coughing spells. It was only interrupted by her high-pitched, loud gasps as she desperately inhaled air. It went on for ten minutes. She was sure all those in the waiting room, every patient and employee who heard the unremitting coughing wanted her to stop long before she finally managed to calm down.

Dr. Ramsey flung the door open, and instead of his customary greeting, he asked "Was that you who were coughing?" Seeing Marsha's flushed face and head bop, he continued, "My, that was impressive. I didn't know you had such a bad cough."

"You didn't? What do you mean you didn't know? This is why I have been coming to you for three years. This is what I keep telling you. Don't you recall I told you twice I passed out because I coughed so much that I could not get air? Don't tell me you never heard me."

"Well, it doesn't matter now", he said, brushing her complaints aside. "Let's see, my nurse will make an appointment for a bronchoscopy and a biopsy. She will schedule an appointment for you at the hospital. In the meantime, get a chest X-ray and a pulmonary function test."

Instantly the physician awakened in Marsha. For the first time she protested in a soft but firm voice: "No, we are not going to take a haphazard approach. There is no point in using a machine gun in the hope that one or the other bullet may hit the target." She felt guessing was over, and it was time to get serious. If Dr. Ramsey was not thinking logically, she would. She had enough of his sweet talk. She needed treatment now.

She asked for either a PET scan or a CT scan of the chest and nixed Ramsey's recommendations. A chest X-ray was only a screening, preliminary test, and it was obvious that she had some underlying disease. *Skip the basic fishing and get to a test which brings a definitive proof,* she thought. A biopsy would be good if only he knew what he needed to biopsy. Without any directions just based on a vague and general suspicion and searching blindly in her lung for a nebulous possibility most likely would result in missing the critical area. After all, he had no idea what lurked in her lung and where it was hiding. Because he didn't know any better, the procedure alone would satisfy him that he did everything, even if he failed to detect something deadly only to surface later. No, no more speculations. She insisted on the PET scan and that was final. At the end, Dr. Ramsey grudgingly agreed, "OK, if that's what you want, get a PET scan."

No one called her with the results, which in itself meant good news. When she called, the receptionist flatly announced that every patient had to make an appointment to learn what her test showed, no one was an exception. Marsha was not alarmed. She figured being colleagues, if there were any bad news Dr. Ramsey wouldn't play with her life and squander what may be valuable time. He would either have phoned her immediately or have told her in person when he had seen her in the hospital. The receptionist only could give her an appointment for two weeks later.

That visit was when she got her death sentence.

With an expression of concern and sadness, Dr. Ramsey revealed to her: "I am sorry, but the PET scan showed a highly reactive mass in the right lower lobe." Then he proceeded to tell her that there was a nearby reactive lymph node in the mediastinum which probably represented a metastasis. Furthermore, there was another mass in the right upper lobe which also looked like a metastasis. He concluded in evident despair, "Frankly, it does not look good."

Marsha was stunned. She clearly heard what the man said, she understood every word. In spite of that, she was stupefied over how calm she remained. She could lucidly think. She didn't dissolve in a pool of tears. Yet, she had just been diagnosed with metastatic lung cancer. She looked around telling herself to remember the room – all the details, the date, the time – forever. It was as if she wanted to stop time by carving every tiny detail into her memory of this moment for all the times to come.

What was there to ask? Maybe the next step? Biopsy? Surgery? Both? She felt somehow disconnected from her body. It was almost as if she were two distinctly separate persons. One was sitting in front of Dr. Ramsey and the other was sitting somewhere in the room, watching her. One was Marsha Redcliff, a patient, and the other was Marsha Redcliff, MD, a physician. She mentally talked to herself as she did to her patients: "*Let's think logically now and ask some intelligent questions.*"

She heard her own soft, steady voice asking him: "OK, let's see. Who would do the biopsy? I really don't know anyone from surgery, but I know first we need to confirm the findings by pathology."

"Well, Dr. Murphy or Dr. Herman could do it," he said. She recognized Murphy's name and completely tuned out the rest. She agreed that Dr. Murphy should do the biopsy.

The procedure went uneventfully. The only disturbing discovery came from Dr. Murphy. As soon as his computer screen showed the image of her chest CT, he turned to Marsha: "Of course, the lesion was already there a year ago." He pointed to a white smudge, about the size of a small lima bean.

"See?" Then seeing the shock on her face, he asked, "You did not know?"

In the interim, he proceeded to measure the smudge with a small ruler while he continued his monologue, "There was no way it could be missed. It's big enough that even if you were not trained to see these images, you would realize the area was not normal."

He looked at his ruler and remarked, "Yep, just as I thought: 1.6 cm in diameter. Hard to miss something that big. Of course now the PET scan shows that it has doubled in size. That's about how much a malignancy can grow in a year. Almost fifteen months really." Then he looked at her: "Why didn't you come for a biopsy sooner?"

Marsha answered with some difficulty. Her mouth was dry and her head reeled with Dr. Murphy's finding. "Why? Because I was told my CT was OK. I am telling you this is what I was told in Dr. Ramsey's office. Do you think I would have neglected it if I had known what was going on? I am neither suicidal nor my own worst enemy."

He shook his head in disbelief but did not continue questioning the decision made by another physician even though he obviously disagreed with the doctor. He turned to Marsha with the calm demeanor of a professional, "Let me say this: it is highly unusual to miss this finding. I don't understand it. Regardless, let's see what can be done now. That's my job and I will do everything I can for you. Today is Friday. How about we do the biopsy on the coming Monday, in the University Hospital. I don't want to waste any time. Is this all right with you?"

"Of course. The sooner, the better."

The hospital's surgical suite and adjoining recovery room were cold. When Marsha became aware of her surroundings and could recognize Dr. Murphy's voice, the procedure had long been completed. She had no memory of it but apparently it went on without a hitch. Dr. Murphy took two samples, one from the lower and one from the upper lobes of her right lung. She had no pain or shortness of breath afterward. Just to be on the cautious side, Dr. Murphy called her in the evening and early next morning to inquire about how she felt.

The following day, shortly after lunch, he called her with the preliminary pathology results. "As predicted, it was cancer. At least the lower lobe lesion was. Adenocarcinoma of the lung. The upper lobe might be something else. It did not look like a metastasis. As soon as I get the report I will call you."

Indeed, he called her after work with the good news: "The second biopsy was not cancer. Looked like an infection. Probably will know more tomorrow. The first one was definitely a malignancy. You know it has to come out as soon as possible. Do you have a surgeon in mind?"

"No, not really. The ones I know at Cecilia Beach Hospital I would prefer not to operate on me. Do you have any recommendation? Perhaps from the University Hospital?"

"Yes, call Dr. Michael Verdi. He is superb. You will like him."

After inquiring about Dr. Verdi and hearing only praise for his work and talent, Marsha called his office for an appointment. As soon as his receptionist learned the reason for seeing the thoracic surgeon, she apologized, "I'm so sorry, Dr. Verdi is in surgery for the whole day today. Could he see you tomorrow at noon? He could examine you during his lunch break."

Marsha thought she heard the woman wrong. Never in her experience did it ever happen that anyone got an appointment within twenty-four hours as a new patient; certainly not during the doctor's lunchtime. Would it be possible, just maybe, that Dr. Murphy and Dr. Verdi realized the urgency of her case, while Dr. Ramsey did not? No, it could not be true, or could it? Neither surgeon knew her, neither worked with her before, yet, they both were concerned with her condition. On the other hand, Dr. Ramsey who was her colleague and claimed to be her friend, never seemed to pay attention to her complaints and even now failed to call her.

Dr. Verdi's nurse hesitatingly asked her, "Didn't you used to have an office on Main Street in the black granite building?"

"Yes, I did." She replied without being flabbergasted, as many people knew her in the area.

"My husband has been one of your patients. He had Guillain-Barre disease. You managed to treat his illness and did all his EMG studies. He wanted to continue his care with you after he got well, but you had left by then."

Her unusual French name and the memory of her husband's infallible faith invested in this uncomfortable test instantly brought to her mind the old days. "Of course I recall him. It was about seven years ago, am I correct? Is he doing well now?"

"Yes, thanks to you. He always praised your work and likes you. Are you back in the area now?"

Dr. Verdi entered and his nurse quietly closed the door behind herself.

Marsha took a good look at him. He was tall, handsome, and a softly spoken man. Kindness and empathy radiated from his face and eyes. His slacks had a knife-like crease, his belt and shoes matched, and his shoes were shined to reflect the ceiling lights. His shirt and tie complimented his salt-and-pepper hair. Marsha breathed easier seeing the neat physician because, in her opinion, the condition of the hands and shoes as well as the general cleanliness told her a lot about a person. These details however, were only superficial compared to his opening sentence.

"I looked at your CT and PET scan. I have printed out some of the pictures so we can discuss them better."

He spread out several pages on his desk, all facing Marsha. "Unfortunately, they were correct. Here is the tumor in question. It was present on the CT scan before and it looks like it had doubled by the time the PET scan was done. This certainly is how a malignancy behaves. Dr. Murphy also confirmed it by phone."

"Oh, then you know him? Did you talk to him recently?" She asked.

"Of course. I worked with him before. He is a good man. I called him to get his opinion and findings."

"I see. You certainly do your homework," Marsha smiled with appreciation.

"That's part of what I do. You would not like it any other way, would you?" He returned her smile.

Marsha was taken aback by his thoroughness and pleasant manners. *Good Lord,* she thought, *this man did not order any of my tests. Therefore, he is not the person responsible for the outcome. That was Dr. Ramsey's duty. Dr. Ramsey who did not tell me I had a mass in my lung and allowed the malignancy to grow and most likely to metastasize. Dr. Ramsey who demanded an office visit two weeks later just to reveal me the PET scan results. On the other hand, Dr. Verdi gave me an urgent appointment and even before he laid his eyes on me, he had reviewed my medical records, viewed all my films, and consulted both Dr. Murphy and the pathologist.* Truly, she liked and respected him.

Dr. Verdi was forthright and direct, yet his tone remained gentle. "I could schedule your operation for the coming Tuesday. You would be the first on my schedule so you would not have to wait and worry. During the surgery the hospital pathologist would see the samples to make sure all edges are clean of the tumor. Most likely the whole lower lobe and the surrounding lymph nodes will have to be removed. I don't know about the upper lobe yet. It depends on what I find there. It may be only partially resected, but if I find malignancy there too, the whole right lung will have to come out. I really hope it will not be necessary. Your outcome would be far better with less radical surgery."

After a brief pause he added, "I feel so bad for you. Being in this predicament, my heart went out for you. I want to do everything I can for a colleague. We should not waste time. I promise, I will do everything I can."

Marsha Redcliff realized the proposed surgery was a must. Even though it was bad news, it was good to hear it from Dr. Verdi and hear it so calmly and clearly stated. All along she felt as if his warm care were blanketing her. She felt comfortable with him and trusted him. At one point during the discussion she looked up just to spot an abstract painting on his office wall. In the chaos of shapeless colors there was a Bible quotation written on the canvas: "I will be with you and walk ahead of you."

She relaxed and knew she had found her surgeon.

15

*It is discouraging to think how many people are
shocked by honesty and how few by deceit.*

———

Noël Coward

The hospital had a group of three general neurologists in
the adjoining building. All three hated hospital work and
refused it as often as they dared. Finally, the hospital forced
them to hire an exclusive neuro-hospitalist. Everyone
felt sorry for Dr. Pacheco, because she was under the
directions of the group, yet, all her functions were ruled
by the hospital. Since the hospital administration and
the group chairman were at odds with each other, the
new neurologist had to navigate every day with extreme
caution so as not to step on any toes. Fortunately, there
was a colleague to assist her in this nightmare maze of
daily work.

Lately, Dr. Pacheco had not a minute of peace. Her
workload doubled since Dr. Redcliff took a few days off
for personal reasons. She did not know why her colleague
was away, only Mr. Lawler was privileged to know her
reasons, and he promised not to reveal it until Dr. Redcliff
was ready to do so. So conscientious Dr. Pacheco came
in early and left away after the sun set until she attended
every neuro care patient. If her pager did not demand

her attention then either the nurses requested her or Sarah called her cell phone with some nonsense.

Sarah, the CEO's secretary, had a one-year junior college education which she compensated with advanced street smarts and an insatiable thirst for power. Nothing was hindering her in pursuing her ultimate goal of becoming an executive administrative assistant of the hospital. Even Dr. Redcliff warned her new colleague to stay out of Sarah's way as much as she could because Sarah operated underhandedly and was vicious.

"Just so you know who you are dealing with, let me tell you what I have heard about her," Marsha started the education. "Her husband divorced her, but when you get to know her you would have to agree with him. Anyway, before their divorce was finalized, he met a woman and apparently fell in love with her. He was foolish enough to appeal to Sarah not to drag out the divorce and in return he promised to agree to all her demands."

"Why? Did he want to marry his new love as soon as the divorce was finalized? Was she pregnant already?" Pacheco interjected.

"Of course he wanted to marry her. And no, she was not pregnant. As a matter of fact they did not have any children though married for several years now. What the sucker did not put into the equation was Sarah's thirst for revenge. He gave her everything, the house, the car, the bank account, and the good Lord knows what else but nothing was enough for her. She wanted revenge."

"I was under the impression she was glad to get rid of him. I overheard Sarah just the other day repeated it to one of the guys in the Doctor's Lounge. Actually, she was funny. Wickedly funny. Someone asked her whether she had any pets, like a cat or a dog. She replied, 'I used to have a dog, but I divorced him.' Marsha, you were there too, didn't you hear it?"

"Yes, I've heard her say it before, but it means nothing. Anybody can say anything and not mean it. Forget the words. Always look at the actions, they don't lie. Contrary to what Sarah projected about her divorce, she was crazy with jealousy. So when her soon to be ex-husband's posters were erected all over the city..."

Pacheco interrupted the story, "Posters? What do you mean 'posters'? Did he run for some office?"

"When his posters to become the School District's Superintendent were erected all over the city," Marsha continued unperturbed, "Sarah went into action. Whatever she did, I don't know. I only saw her flashing a new ring on her hand in the office and laugh, 'Who says blackmail does not pay?' Suddenly, all the posters were removed and her ex withdrew his application for the post." Marsha finished the account by imitating with her hand a knife slicing her throat.

"Whoa, that's heavy-duty stuff." Dr. Pacheco was impressed.

"So, just do like I do: stay away from her and don't fall for her charm. She would attempt to be your best buddy, to look out for you and represent you to the administration but as soon as she leaves you, you have to check your back to remove the knife she stuck in you. Don't ever underestimate her; she is the most unscrupulous witch since the Wicked Witch of the West. And you are no Dorothy, either." Marsha warned her.

Sarah's self-importance was evident with every phone contact she made. She demanded an immediate response, and when Pacheco protested, claiming her priorities were the patients; Sarah snapped at her, "I pay you to do what I tell you first."

Dr. Pacheco was so shocked by the rude and blatant attack that only after Sarah left did it occur to her what her response should have been. She angrily thought she should have told Sarah, that as a secretary, she did not pay her. Her paycheck came from the neurology group.

Next morning Dr. Pacheco requested a meeting with her group's chief and indignantly complained of the secretary overstepping her boundaries. After all, she was a highly specialized physician who efficiently did her job and under no circumstances would accept this kind of treatment. She reasoned that only the physicians were generating primary income in the hospital. Actually, a physician's signature authorized all interventions, including nursing care, therapists, laboratory and other diagnostics, medical equipment, and supplies. All non-physician employees such as nurses, technicians, kitchen and maintenance personnel, and all the administrative staff were paid from these revenues and from charging exorbitant fees for medications and supplies. Therefore, a secretary most certainly should not ever act as if she were an irreplaceable wheel in this giant machinery. Personally and professionally Dr. Pacheco was offended and called for further intervention.

Her chief, Dr. Marlene immediately contacted Mr. Lawler and formally requested an apology. He emphasized Dr. Pacheco was hired and paid by his group and not the hospital. In return, the CEO called to his attention the very fact that the hospital granted a monthly stipend to cover the neurologist's salary. Mr. Lawler's subtle questioning of Dr. Marlene's leadership and control over his group made the physician uneasy. After all, no one was irreplaceable, as the CEO casually remarked. At the end nothing was resolved and if possible, the rift deepened between them further.

Just to be on the safe side, Mr. Lawler touched base with the legal department, too. He felt it was important to pre-emptively alert the hospital's higher echelon of the possible trouble makers. In his view both Dr. Marlene and Dr. Pacheco could cause serious complications in the future. By notifying the legal department, Mr. Lawler delegated his full responsibility for any conceivable upsetting development. From the moment he shared his concerns with the legal department, the potential threat became the lawyers' problem.

To the CEO's satisfaction the chief of the legal division responded without delay: Mr. Lawler had been summoned to a meeting to discuss various ways and methods to implement tighter control over the physicians. A proposal to strip the medical staff of any decision making was set into motion straight away. The attorney suggested to increase the physician's patient load which, in return, should prevent them from having free time to discuss non-medical topics. After all, their job was to take care of the patients and nothing else. If necessary, the attorney even projected a needed swift repercussion by making a disciplinary example which would deter others from being too vocal. Simultaneously, he instructed Mr. Lawler to smooth over the ruffled feathers, keep a cheerful and friendly communication with the doctors, and report any and all response to the quietly implemented new policy.

As soon as Mr. Lawler hung up the phone, Sarah stepped forward from his doorway. She carefully avoided mentioning that she stood by the door and listened to her boss' entire conversation before she decided it was time to reveal herself. Sarah always recognized a situation which could be used to her best interest. Now she grabbed the opportunity to straighten out both men. She only said it must have been a sheer coincidence that she happened to come by and overheard part of the discussion.

"I am so sorry Mr. Lawler that you were called on the carpet by Dr. Marlene. I don't know where he gets the nerve to question a CEO."

"He complained about you Sarah. You should lay off his employees or go through me if you have anything to discuss. I hope you realize, the direct approach is not beneficial to your longevity here." The warning was very ominous.

Sarah swiftly changed tactics. She appeared to be humble and defenseless, "I am so hurt to be insulted by Dr. Marlene when all I did was try to protect you from him. I thought I could talk to Dr. Pacheco woman-to-woman in the hope she might talk to her boss. I have been told she might be a bit too friendly, a bit too close to Dr. Marlene. I didn't know what they meant, but whatever their relationship might be, I've tried to use it to your advantage. I am not surprised at Dr. Marlene, he probably would deny it. But Dr. Pacheco? Apparently I misjudged her. So sorry about it."

"What do you mean you were trying to protect me from Dr. Marlene?" The CEO demanded with raised eyebrows. He did not seem to be so threatening any more. He rather showed curiosity blended with confusion.

"You probably don't know Dr. Marlene wanted to be a CEO as soon as the position became a bit shaky for Dr. Jamison. I think they were good friends anyway and Dr. Jamison practically promised the position to him. He groomed Dr. Marlene to be his successor. They just never imagined Dr. Jamison would have to leave so unexpectedly and you were immediately named for his position. I bet this is what's in the background." Sarah went for the jugular. She had no knowledge of any closeness between Jamison and Dr. Marlene, just as she never heard any gossip about Pacheco and her boss, but she realized neither would be approached to validate her statements. She felt safe to accuse them.

"I don't believe this was the reason for his call. Although, I definitely sensed some hostility in his tone. Regardless,

I appreciate you defending me, but please be more diplomatic in the future." Mr. Lawler was no longer the original heavy-weight he presented and Sarah noted the change with satisfaction.

"Of course, I will. Thank you for your support. You are absolutely the right man for this position: not only smart but also fair and just. I appreciate you."

On her way out she sort of hesitated then seemed to gather enough courage to turn back to Mr. Lawler and said, "In return for you defending me I promise always to warn you about what Dr. Marlene is up to because I know him. I am positive he would not rest as long as you are the CEO; he has enough to cover up on his own. After what he does whole day long, I have no idea how he has any time left for his work, for his patients."

"Oh? Do you know something that I don't? Or something you didn't tell me," questioned the number one man of the hospital as he looked up. If anyone should be aware of what was going on in his workplace, it was him. Maybe Sarah would be a good source of the news.

"Well, Dr. Marlene has enough to hide to keep him busy until the cows come home. How he finds time for work between doing every household shopping and chasing the nurses too, I have no idea. Didn't you ever see the infamous couch in his office? It opens up to a queen size bed. Surely he doesn't need one to rest at work. Unfortunately, these habits are expensive. I guess everything cost money and the rumor mill says he may be dipping in the company kitty."

"Where did you get this information? Is it a fact or only gossip?"

"I wouldn't know Mr. Lawler, but think logically. Dr. Marlene has two kids in private college, his wife does not work, and she did not inherit a fortune before. Dr. Marlene wasn't independently wealthy, either. To finance their affluent life style on his salary is impossible. Maybe if he had yours..." Sarah let the words dangle in her boss' mind and retreated to her desk.

When alone she took out her secret notebook she started on the day she met Mr. Lawler and made another entry. Who knows when she could use the information she gathered about her boss? When you have something to sell and it is of rare quality, you can always find a buyer. Naturally, the price would be negotiable.

16

Confidence in an unfaithful man in time
of trouble is like a broken tooth,
and a foot out of joint.

Proverbs 27:19

Ten days after the biopsy and eight days after she was given the diagnosis by the pathologist, Dr. Redcliff finally got an appointment with Dr. Ramsey. The previous two weeks had been tense. Although she had experienced disbelief, shed tears over her ultimate loss, and felt anger at her failing body, she appeared calm and collected as if this were just a casual visit. Marsha Redcliff realized what she had to face.

Dr. Ramsey read the papers he held in his hands then told her what she already knew: "I am really sorry to say but the biopsy showed adenocarcinoma of the lung. Remember, I told you before that this was the most likely diagnosis. They don't know about the lymph nodes yet, but there is most likely the same cancer. Metastases, of course. I am so sorry." He looked solemn and sad as if he were at a funeral.

Marsha marveled at his smooth talk and his sad expression. Boy, he was good at it! She wondered how frequently he had said those words; how many times he had given the same death sentence to patients. She pondered on how often he had covered his missed diagnosis and if he ever thought of the role he played in her condition. She would have loved to read his mind, not just listened to his flowing words.

He easily continued, "So, let's see what should be your next step. Naturally, you know you'll need surgery. I need to think about who could do it. I'll do some research and contact some friends and get back to you with my recommendation by the end of next week. Then you could make an appointment and see the surgeon. Don't worry, in 4-6 weeks, everything should be done. You know I am your friend, above all. I want to help you."

Marsha's cold voice cut into the syrupy sweetness, "It won't be necessary, thank you. I have already contacted Dr. Michael Verdi, the thoracic surgeon."

"You did? When? How could you? I have only just given you the diagnosis!"

"Yes, you did," she agreed, "But Dr. Murphy and the pathologist gave me the diagnosis ten days ago. They advised me immediately to act as there was no time to waste and play with my life." Marsha looked straight in his eyes but saw no signs of shock or regrets on his face. It remained impassive. She continued, "I have decided on Dr. Verdi doing my surgery and have seen him already. Any objections?"

"Oh no, he is good. No objections at all. Yes, he probably would be the best. I like Michael. He is a good guy. Let me call him for you."

Marsha could not help but admire how quickly Dr. Ramsey could turn a situation around and regain control, getting over a set-back.

"It won't be necessary. Thanks, just the same. As I said, I have already met Dr. Verdi and he has scheduled my surgery for Tuesday."

"But that's in four days! Well in that case, let me refer you to a good oncologist for chemo. You will need it after the surgery."

"No thanks. No referral now. Not yet. Let's get over the surgery first. Besides, I don't think they use much chemo for a lung adenocarcinoma any more but switched rather to immunotherapy nowadays. If anything, I probably will need that."

"Yes, yes of course," He mumbled and turned to look at the PET scan images. He clearly was confused by her sudden assertiveness. Scanning the images was something he, as a pulmonologist, could do and share with her. "Aha, here it is: this is the cancer. What a shame! It's pretty impressive, don't you think? Thank goodness *I* ordered the PET scan. Imagine *if you let it go* further!" His desperate attempts to blame the victim were aimed to conceal his obvious oversight.

Marsha was stunned to silence hearing Dr. Ramsey blatantly twisting the facts. She stood paralyzed, only her mind raced with the speed of light. If the size of the cancer was so impressive, how come he missed it? Why hadn't he seen it sixteen months ago and sent her to get the proper care? It was he who had ignored it and thus had let the cancer grow and spread. He delayed telling her the diagnosis and wasted precious time when all the other doctors treated her with urgency. And now he had shamelessly claimed credit for ordering the correct diagnostic test? Had he forgotten or thought she had amnesia to recall it was not him but Marsha who had requested the PET scan? He had only wanted a chest X-ray, a pulmonary function test, and a blind procedure of bronchoscopy and biopsy from an unknown location of an undiagnosed possible lesion.

At the end, he dared to declare himself to be her savior when in reality he had been negligent all along. His pitiful attempt of lame damage control in truth merited criminal negligence. For him, to presume that she did not care about her own health and life and that only his alertness saved her from a certain demise was a slap in the face. Was not it she who tried to get help for the symptoms of coughing for three years? Was not she the one who took everything he ordered then objected to each being ineffective? And he dared to point a finger at her to be responsible for her illness. Marsha felt as a rape victim must have felt in Court: after the physical insult, she had to endure a humiliating public mental rape too.

Dr. Ramsey, not realizing what swirled behind Marsha's unemotional face and clearly overflowed by sympathy and touched by his own syrupy words stepped closer to hug her.

Marsha instantly stiffened and became immobile, unable to return the kind gesture. She conscientiously noted the awkward situation and was puzzled by her lack of response. Being an extrovert and a true-and-tried, touchy-feely gal, this uncomfortable half-a-hug was a first for her. Just as cancer was a first for her, too.

On her way out she stopped at the receptionist's desk only to request a copy of her records. She decided never to return to Dr. Ramsey's office. Being in the health care field she was aware of unscrupulous physicians adding modifications to old entries in the patient's chart. Her gut reaction told her that this was her only chance to preserve the truth in her records. She opted to shun him even before she had read what was written in his notes.

Once at home, she scanned the pages of her medical record into her computer. She read each page as she fed it into the scanner. To say she became dumbfounded reading the entries would be a gross understatement.

The original chest CT interpretation was signed by Dr.

H. Katsui, a reputable radiologist and co-owner of the Unlimited Concepts of Imaging in Cecilia Beach. Marsha Redcliff frequently referred her clinic patients to them and never had problems with their reports. True, in her almost paranoid fear of possibly missing something and being potentially sued by anyone, she not only read the report in its entirety but reviewed every film herself.

Reading Dr. Katsui's conclusion, she bitterly laughed at herself: she did not trust him fully with her patients and reviewed his work; yet she took his word at face value when it came to her own body. Then she topped this by believing Dr. Ramsey's evaluation: "Everything is the same. Nothing new was seen." Yet, unbeknownst to her, Dr. Katsui never made a definite statement, just recommended a further study of what he described as "bands of linear consolidation or possible mucus plug." He made absolutely no reference to the right lower lobe lesion.

Marsha bitterly whispered, "Yeah, he sure added the customary cliché at the end, a 'Comparison to prior CT or a contrast study may be beneficial.' Dr. Katsui learned to protect his assets, just like every other physician did who lived in our litigious society.

What she could not explain was how Katsui missed the tumor in her lower lobe. He was an excellent radiologist and this was a huge lesion, not easy to overlook. Maybe he was interrupted during the dictation and forgot about it when he returned to finish it, she guessed. Then she instantly scolded herself for trying to find excuses to the very man who fatally wronged her. It was time to get rid of the Goody-Goody-Two-Shoes personality and become Dr. Spicy again.

Next she reviewed Dr. Ramsey's notes. Finally, in his next to last office visit dictation she found the proverbial smoking gun: "Unfortunately, *we were unable to pull up the images of the CAT* scan due to some problems with the program of Unlimited Concepts. We will try to obtain the CD and review the film. We will give her a prescription for the vest to provide mucus clearing." So it was not true what the nurse practitioner and Dr. Ramsey told her. They never reviewed the film and actually only assumed it was negative. Yet, she was told for a fact that her CT was normal.

It was spelled out in black and white, right in front of her, that her pulmonologist and his assistant knowingly and deliberately misrepresented the test results. If that alone didn't lead to enough injury then they topped it by neglecting to follow up and act upon the incomplete results. Did they jeopardize her health as a direct consequence of the carelessness? Did they endanger her life? Did they increase her surgical risk and make her more vulnerable by allowing the cancer to spread? You can bet your last red cent they did.

In reviewing her own medical records Marsha realized the sequence of errors and gross neglect. First the radiologist missed the tumor and made a vague reference to an obscure finding in the text of description. Then he omitted it in the conclusion of the interpretation. The pulmonologist got the report and read the conclusion only. Being pressed for time, he disregarded reviewing the films himself. He guessed the chronic cough being the same this test was not different from the prior ones, either.

Marsha checked the visit date on her calendar and discovered it was on the day before Thanksgiving. Suddenly, it became clear how every other detail contributed to the disastrous outcome. The day before the holiday everyone was in a hurry to get home and prepare for the feast. In the high volume of patient load, no one was paying attention to details. At least the assistant noted the skipped review of the CT and probably planned to do it when the office opened up on the following Monday. But, by then they forgot about it. Apparently, her chart was opened next when she had returned for her yearly follow up. If she didn't have the coughing spells then and there, and if she did not insist on having a PET scan, then next she would have detected some sign of advanced, metastatic lung cancer followed by a predictable death. What a "perfect storm" it was! Every detail contributed to and worsened the scenario. It was a flawless *circulus vitiosus*. The domino-effect was due to an easily avoidable initial error which might cost her life now.

During this discovery, Marsha got angrier by the minute. She thought she might need anger management, but then she decided all she needed was increased tolerance for the idiots in her life. What she prayed for was more patience and not more strength, for if she got strength, she might as well ask for bail-money, too.

How could her colleague treat her like this? If this was how he cared for a fellow physician, what did he do to an everyday John Doe coming off the streets? How could he sleep with clear conscience when he never looked at her films and discharged her for a whole year with a half-inch mass in her lung? Then she remembered what Rabbi Teitelbaum said long ago, "If one does not have a conscience, it does not bother him. We could only be sorry for him." Marsha was so hurt and mad that she could not feel sorry for either the radiologist or the pulmonologist.

This was beyond the point of a discussion. Whatever a doctor did not know the lawyers knew better in the Court room. For the first time it occurred to Marsha Redcliff that she might need a malpractice attorney.

17

*In every winter's heart there is a quivering spring,
and behind the veil of each night there is a smiling dawn.*

_____

Kahlil Gibran

As soon as she heard her initial diagnosis of cancer, Marsha became numb. This was not what she expected. She had no risk factors, never had been a smoker, and never had been exposed to second-hand smoking. She had not been near agricultural chemicals, or Agent Orange. Her ex-husband was overtly careful and repeatedly tested their properties for radon. At the beginning of their marriage, he even refused to buy a house, because they detected radon prior to completing the purchase. There was no family history of lung cancer. So where did this come from? The word "cancer" itself was scary and her medical knowledge made it by far more terrifying.

Her knowledge of solid tumors came from her studies and work, the fascinating reading of malignancies. Once upon a time she wanted to be a physician who specialized in lung cancer. Now she recalled the Chinese proverb, "Be careful what you covet, because if the gods want to punish you they might fulfill your wish." She thought of the irony of becoming a doctor, but becoming a doctor with lung cancer. That's what happens if you don't make your wish in Chinese, she laughed bitterly.

So, the final diagnosis was lung cancer. The word echoed over and over in her mind as if she could not believe it and needed to convince herself. The physician in her kept repeating "*I have lung cancer.*" Then she added "*and I have two additional metastases. That means at least a Stage III, although Dr. Ramsey told me it most likely was a Stage IV, the stage before death claimed its victim.*" His words were burnt into her memory; his voice forever in her head as he finished his talk, "You are a doctor. You know what happens then. We can do only so much, then that's it."

This is when the word "death" hit her. It hit her with all its frightening reality. Instantly the scientist took over her mind. So what was death? Cessations of all life functions. Destruction of an organism. She recalled learning about it in pathology, hearing about it in various medical lectures. Oh hell, no! Who cares about science! It was not an organism, this time it was Marsha Redcliff, a person. It was her body, her life, and not a chapter in a text book she read. It was she who faced death, annihilation, demise, fatality, obliteration. The final exit. The end. Would she be able to do it? Sure. Was she given any other choices? No. She had to bear it. There was no rehearsal, no trial, only the final curtain. No one was given a chance to practice how to die when the time came. She just had to wing it. Somehow she had to go on and do the best she could.

The repeated word eventually lost its shock value and became her new reality. All right, she thought, so she will die. Everyone dies sooner or later. Why would she be an exception? She was the same as everyone else. What would make her special? Nothing. It did not matter what she did, how much she studied, what car she drove, or where she lived. Doctors got ill, too, and eventually they also died. Nobody got a promise to go to Heaven on his own two feet, alive.

She repeatedly assured herself that death was just a momentary meeting and there was nothing to fear. After all, while she was still alive death was not present, and by the time it arrived, she would already be gone. They would only meet for a fleeting moment to change places. She could deal with that moment. What bothered her was the road she was to be forced to travel to reach that moment.

No one suspected her illness in the hospital. Anyone looking at her saw a peaceful, almost contemplative physician who concentrated on her work. She appeared as someone who had not a single concern or worries on this earth, but probably only was seriously focusing on something. Being a neurologist, she most likely had a complicated case the nurses decided and left her alone. No one suspected the raging confusion, the stormy bewilderment, and all the twirling chaotic thoughts that hid behind her cool façade and coiled up in her mind in the death grip of a giant anaconda.

One of the neighbors who learned about Marsha's predicament admired her calm demeanor, "You are amazing, my dear. Only a doctor could accept this tight spot as you do. You are my hero. I wish I could be more like you and take things less personally."

Marsha just stared at her stupefied, literally unable to utter a word. Who could ever get the idea that doctors have no emotions? Didn't people ever realize doctors were human? If she could weep with patients when giving them the news of their incurable illness, wouldn't she sob over her own death sentence? How much more "personal" could an illness get but be terminal? She could not even respond to her neighbor.

All she wanted to do was cry, yet, forced herself not

to show she was hurting. She figured life had a tendency to bring enough problems to everyone. Truly life did not need anyone's help and most of all she did not need to contribute to its quandary. She kept repeating in her mind: *"No tears. Not now. Don't you dare! Don't let anyone see you cry. Later, when you are alone, you can cry as much as you want. But not now. Not yet. Not yet."*

"Dr. Redcliff do you have a moment?" Josè's voice brought her back to reality. "Sarah, Mr. Lawler's body guard is on the line for you."

"For me? What could she want from me? Did she say anything?" Marsha picked up the flashing line while simultaneously noting Josè's facial expression indicated he was just as much in the dark as she was.

"Good, I need to talk to Mr. Lawler, anyway. I will be right there," She said as she picked up her stethoscope and reflex hammer. "Josè, I'll be back shortly, I have to go to Administration. Save my tuning fork for me, I think I left it in Bed 4."

Mr. Lawler welcomed her with opened doors and after a couple of meaningless niceties, immediately started: "I was told you were a guest speaker on the Miami Medical Convention last year. We were invited to give a speech to the medical school staff and students next week. I would like you to do it, Dr. Redcliff."

Marsha raised up her hands in protest but the CEO continued as if he did not notice her aversion.

"I am close friends and golf buddies with the Dean of the Medical School and he asked for my help. I cannot very well refuse his request, can I?" He looked at Marsha, expecting her to agree with him. She remained silent and only her eyes followed the CEO as he walked up and down behind his desk.

"The Dean wanted to educate the new generation of physicians on real life encounters with patients and also how it affects the physicians. He wanted it kept somewhat on the light side, shall I say, sort of entertaining? I have to agree with him that laughter would stick to the students' minds better while they learned a good lesson from it. Do you agree, Dr. Redcliff?"

Not waiting for her to answer, he continued, "So I asked around and discovered your speech was similar. Am I correct? In that case you wouldn't have to write another one. Would you do it?"

Marsha slowly responded, "I could give you my speech, it's on my computer, but I would not be able to do it. Maybe you could read it Mr. Lawler. It does not matter to the students who they hear it from, I am sure."

"You could have the day off Dr. Redcliff. Someone will take care of your patients, don't worry." The CEO was jovially smiling as he eagerly assured her.

"That's good, because I was just about asking for a few months of leave of absence. I will need surgery next week."

"Oh my, I hope nothing serious." He clearly was waiting for Marsha to tell him some minor female operation.

"I am afraid it is Mr. Lawler. I was just diagnosed with a mass in my lung. It has to come out. I will let you know later what it turned out to be." She smiled at the surprised administrator. "I will give my paper to Sarah tomorrow so you can review it. Isn't that funny, I just wrote it up in the form to be published. All it needs is someone like you with a clear voice to read it. It's ready to go."

One task off of her checklist, her work was notified. At least this was easy, she thought. Telling it to her children and friends was going to be much harder. She decided to face them without being too sentimental. "Just the facts Ma'am, just the facts," as Sergeant Friday said long ago in his TV show. No one should remember her being a slushy-mushy tear bag.

Her friends represented memories from various stages of her life. Some came from her previous work places and some were ex-neighbors. She recalled her grandmother pressed flowers in her prayer book from special bouquets or occasions. She gathered people for the same reason. So many memories they shared, so much they experienced together! A gold ribbon of friendship intertwined and connected them. Marsha was thankful for what they brought to her life, by making it more colorful and exciting.

She invited them for dinner and emphasized she had a good reason for it; they should not miss the get-together. After dinner she opened the champagne bottles. Each had a glass in hand waiting for Marsha's toast.

"I just wanted to tell you how much I appreciated each and every one of you. Thank you for being my friend. We already went through a lot together, but now I have to ask for your support again. Next week I will have part of my lung removed for cancer. I need you to stand by me. I am counting on you, don't let me get disappointed!" She smiled through her tears.

No one suspected it, no one expected this. The shock following the toast could be felt as if a tangible net had fallen over them without warning and entangled minds and bodies into a motionless, thoughtless heap. At the end, leaving, each chose a piece of cut crystal or porcelain whatever caught their fancy from Marsha's home. It was fine with her, she probably didn't need it for long, she thought. Only after they were all gone she realized that they left with a small piece from her home, but took a large part of her heart.

18

There is always the danger that we may just do the work for the sake of the work. This is where the respect and the love and the devotion come in.

Mother Teresa of Calcutta

Dear Mr. Lawler:

Enclosed is the print out I promised you the other day. I am sure you will do a terrific job reading it next week. By the way, these are not the real names of the patients, I know the HIPAA regulations, don't worry.

Good luck,
M.R.

PS: let me know how it turned out, will you?

LOST BETWEEN THE SHEETS
Marsha S. Redcliff, MD, MS, FAPBN
Cecilia Beach Community Hospital
Department of Internal Medicine
Division of Neurology and Psychiatry
workingneurons@gmail.com

Lost Between the Sheets

Patients are not like you and me. First of all, they are sick and don't feel well. Second, they are in a hospital which is a totally new surrounding to most of them. Those that are familiar with the hospital are labeled as "frequent flyers" for their innumerable admissions. They don't mind being there. The rest of the patients just want to get better enough to get out of their confinement.

From doctors, through nurses, therapists, dietary personnel and cleaning crew, everybody has access at any time to any room. Even the maintenance man can enter a room to check out or repair something. Of course they all knock, but can a patient say "no" to their entry? Hardly. Usually, the patient has no word in a decision making. Although legally he is expected to be involved, but in practice, no, not really.

Everything is strange in a hospital. The language used is studded with words seldom heard in general speech. Don't you just plain "answer" a question instead of "cognisize" or, even worse, "verbalize" your thoughts? Do you get along with your roommate or do you "develop a meaningful, positive interrelationship and verbal exchange" with her? Now if these are not confusing expressions, you are either a professional patient or too sick to care to find out the true meaning.

In time you learn not to be bothered by unexpected visitors while you get a bed bath in less water than what is used for a baptism. Modesty is tossed out altogether after the attending doctor or nurse assures you that you are fine to sit on the toilet while they talk to you. They wonder why you don't ask more questions about your own condition, but you cannot tell them that all you want is a closed door and some privacy.

At home you sleep in your own bed which you already made comfortable by adjusting all the lumps to your body. Or you have adjusted all your body lumps to the now comfortable mattress. In contrast, the hospital bed squeaks in protest as you roll over because the mattress is covered with washable plastic. The pillow might be as flat as a pancake or brand new and overstuffed with foam rubber. Either way, as you attempt to turn, your head bounces off. The cover is a sheet with a light weight blanket. If you are used to a heavier weight of a cover at home, you are out of luck. Unless your nurse is a compassionate soul with time on her hand, you will have to make do without the extra covers. In other words, a hospital experience is bewildering to say the least.

Now if that's not enough, there are doctors and nurses who like to ask the same questions over and over. They assess and process you. They poke, listen, push, turn, bend, lift and kneed your body as if it were not yours to hurt but theirs to be studied. When they leave you exhausted and finally alone in your room, you start thinking why did you say something and not say something else, wondering what they might think, whether they understood you or just laugh at you now. Yes, at times they laugh and at times they cry for you. I can assure you they are all human and they all laugh and cry. Exactly like you and I do.

Just think of Jarrell Bruckner. Let me tell you, he was a fish out of water when he was admitted to the hospital for the first time in his life. For seventy-three years he lived on his family farm working the land his entire life. He knew everything about planting and harvesting, taking care of his animals, even fixing his tractor. What he did not know was what the effect of cigarettes would be on his lungs and on his legs. He listened to what the hospital people said, but did not understand why they were concerned with his painful legs and how they connected the leg pain to his cigarettes. These sleek city folks did not even want to hear about how he rolled his own cigarettes from the best tobacco leaf that grew on his farm; yet, they claimed this caused his claudication. Whatever claudication meant. Nobody ever explained that to him. He finally tuned out the nurses and the doctors; after all, if they bad-mouthed his cigarettes then they knew nothing of good quality tobacco.

After surgery, his painful legs were worse than ever before, but they told him the pain would subside as the wound healed. They also told him he had to stop smoking which he did not agree with, but kept looking at them without uttering any objection. Then a young girl who looked like his granddaughter but probably was even younger, cheerfully announced: "First we are going to dangle then we could ambulate together. Are you up to the challenge?" Jarrell could not say that his wife of fifty-one years might not agree with this plan and he, himself, did not feel up to it, either. The girl left without the projected activity and he breathed easier without doing any such thing with a young woman. Shameless really, though she was quite pretty, he thought. Could not she find some young fellow to dangle with instead of a married seventy-three year old man?

Or we should recall Miss Beulah Jones. She was admitted with acute abdominal pain. She was told to answer as honestly as she could to all sorts of questions. A man wearing a white coat examined her and asked whether she was sexually active. Miss Beulah was over fifty, married, and most of her life tired to her bones. She truthfully replied: "Sexually active? Oh no dear, I just 'lays' there."

The doctor tried to control himself but finally burst into laughter. "You are a gem! I just love your frank replies!" he said.

Miss Beulah smiled without comprehending what was so funny and why she was complimented on being candid when she was told to be honest.

Then there was a young man who had a seizure and was sleeping it off in the intensive care unit. His fiancée was a well-endowed woman in her early twenties, although it was hard to grasp how anyone could grow breasts that size in twenty years. Half of them could not be hidden in her bra and the low cut blouse revealed her hopeless efforts to squeeze them into captivity. Regardless of the revealing top and her limited schooling she felt responsible for her man's care. She questioned her fiancé's doctor about her medical credentials. "So you are a woman neurologist? Do you know anything about 'seejures'?"

"Yes, I think so."

"But do you know like, what's wrong with him? Because his 'seejures' are like very rare and special, not just the average kind like, you know. They are *Granny 'Seejures'*." She seemed to be pleased with her knowledge and ability to teach this woman who claimed to be a neurologist.

The doctor bit her lips, quickly examined the sleeping man then left the room. She held her laughter until she was out of hearing distance and told every nurse not to call this guy's seizures "grand mal" any more. The fiancée's diagnosis was far better.

Or look at Miss Patricia Taylor. She is an attractive young woman, a pillar of her Southern Baptist church. What she lacks in education she compensates with infallible faith and upright behavior. This is why it strikes me strange that she hides the reason of her prior hospitalization. She only shakes her head in obvious shame and whispers "I cannot say, it is such a nasty disease."

I am sure it was going to turn out to be a sexually transmitted one, so I assured her that I have heard them all, she can tell me. But she still continues to repeat "a nasty, nasty disease" and nothing more. She finally breaks down in huge tears as she almost inaudibly whispers with a strong Mississippi accent "It was a Coxackie disease." Her accent has no "x" but "cks" only. Then with all her shame and profound sincerity she adds through her sobbing "I have no idea how I got it because I am a decent girl, I attend a Baptist church every week and I don't do such things. Never did. It's just plain nasty. But that's what my doctor claimed I had."

I look at her for a minute but cannot control my rising laughter and through the giggles I explain her Coxackie is a virus just like the flu and has nothing to do with what she imagined. The poor soul lived with her undeserved shame and silently suffered in humility. Now she can tell anyone she only had a viral throat infection. She holds her head up and is ready to call back the persistent young man to accept his calls for a date. She is freed of her past and has no more dishonors.

Oh, and you should recall old Mr. Abe Silverman. He was confused and being at the end of the hallway in a private room, was seldom disturbed by the nurses. A nurse's aide reported him having seizures and the night nurse hastily alerted the neurology resident.

On her way the resident quickly scanned but saw nothing alarming on the electroencephalogram monitor. As she entered the room, ice cold air hit her as if they were outdoors in Upper New York in February. The poor old man uncontrollably shivered under a single bed sheet. The thermostat was adjusted from fifty-four to seventy-six degrees and he was covered with a couple of pre-warmed blankets. He thankfully fell asleep in the comfortable warmth.

In the early morning Mrs. Silverman stopped the visiting professor as he was dragging the schlep of residents in tow. She was hysterically complaining of her husband's deteriorating mental condition. She relayed his awful experience: during the night he thought he was put into the morgue, but a white-dressed angel warmed him up and he was back to living again.

Mrs. Silverman could not understand why one of the residents assured her with a wide smile "It might sound incredible, but trust me, this was the only time your husband was not confused. He really is improving."

Yes, there are good reasons to laugh, especially when one reads the patient charts. If the properly documented first post-operative entry reads "Nurse and patient walked the entire hallway, passing flatus freely", wouldn't you be tempted to ask: "Really? Both of them?" Good job. Methane Mama functions again.

But even funnier are the dictations. When it reads an Alzheimer patient "frequently wanders away from home: yet, never got to Lowes", it takes a while to recall the original dictation said "never got lost".

Don't you think some words should not be divided but in their entirety should be transferred to the next line? Instead writing as "the" at the end of one line and continue "rapist" in the next row, just write the whole word "therapist" in the next line. Somehow "therapist" and "the rapist" don't mean the same. Or think of the gynecologist who happily announces in his patient's chart that "Finally we managed her to get pregnant". We don't dare to ask who or what he refers by the word "we" but hope it is the husband and the prescribed hormone therapy.

And as if these were not challenging enough, we have foreign-born doctors. Their accent is hard to understand even when talking face to face and not into a Dictaphone. No wonder, whatever they say can be easily misinterpreted. Most dictations are transcribed elsewhere, some as far as India. After being electronically transferred overseas, the dictation is sent back the same way before appearing in written form on the computer screen. I don't mean to say the transcriptionists don't speak English, but some of the idioms are certainly getting changed along the way. Just imagine the doctor says "Patient was an orphan and he was raised by an aunt." In characteristic Jungle Book style this is transcribed as "the patient was raised by a hound".

Even modern commercials have an impact on a patient's chart. A freshly imported doctor obviously watches enough television to chart "Place of work: Aflac, a duck company".

Of course, we all laugh reading the application of an aspiring nursing assistant. For identifying her gender, she answers to "Sex: Occasionally". Then, as an afterthought, she adds "But only with boyfriend". She proceeds to the next question, "Nearest relative: Mother. Relationship: Mostly good." We conclude she certainly is honest. If she also has a good heart to care for the patients we can train her, no problem.

But these are only errors in writing made by hurrying nurses, overworked doctors or tired transcriptionists. Let's face it, there are plenty of reasons to smile without ever opening a chart. One only needs to look and listen, no commentary is needed. For example, when the hairiest chest is shaved in perfectly round patches to allow attaching the electrodes of an electrocardiogram, you know the man refused to lose all his chest hair. Without most of his virgin wool left intact on his chest, he would feel naked, almost feminine - depending on his chest development, but with the patches he thinks he may pass for a somewhat watered-down Marcello Mastroianni or George Clooney. Perhaps moth attacked, but what the heck! At least the rest of the chest shows the past glory.

We all called him "the Chief" for his Apache chest: a patch of hair here, a patch of hair there...

Laurie Hunter is a chronic pain complainer and frequently gets admitted for intractable migraine headache treatment. We call the hallway the "Laurie Hunter Wing" because by now her insurance paid for not only the expense of building it but also for the upkeep of the rooms and the adjacent hallway. She tells us exactly what medications, how much and how often she should get. She knows it by the milligram. As soon as she awakens, she summons the nurses to her bedside with demands for pain medication.

It is hard to take her claim of pain seriously because her mandates are delivered by slurred speech and half-open eyes. In spite of the obvious drug effect, she hides her incredibly unbearable pain with heroic strength and bravely hides the smallest telltale sign of discomfort. Once she was caught sound asleep with her face in her lunch plate between the mashed potato and corn on the cob. Now we call mashed potato the "Laurie Hunter facial mask".

Occasionally a completely confused man brakes into the hallway without wearing a stitch of clothes. He tosses his designer hospital gown with a flair to the approaching nurse's face as he yells, "I was born naked as a jaybird, I will fly away naked again!" Fly he cannot, but you should see how fast all the nurses can practically fly to cover him up!

Even characteristics linked to a special profession are stamped on a patient. The Wild West's last true cowboy wiggles out of his restraints, turns a pillowcase into a bandanna and dressed in little more than the makeshift scarf and loosened restraints he sneaks into the bathroom. He finds the urine measuring cup and delightfully announces to the visiting medical team

"Hell, this is the smoothest damn whiskey in any saloon, I declare!" His delirium tremens confuses the toilet bowl with a punch bowl and he refills his cup in spite of several strapping young men dragging him away. "Hey, I rode wild mustangs; I can ride your ass..." His voice fades as the medication puts him to sleep.

In the meantime, Dr. Mandel is scrubbed for surgery. He is a good-looking, tall, and a very proper neurosurgeon from Boston. He is emotionless, the epitome of an ivory-tower scientist. Now he stands with his sterile gloved hands raised in the air so as not to touch anything non-sterile. He coolly instructs the nurse to tie his gown, but she accidentally pulls his scrub suit string and his pants slide to his ankles. He cannot grab his pants with his gloved hands and the nurse cannot help him because she is doubled up with laughter. The news travel faster through the entire hospital than a California wildfire: under the custom-made business suit cool-cat Dr. Mandel wears a red G-string for underwear.

In the Intensive Care old Willie Brown is dying of diabetic complications. His last years were like Chinese torture: he lost both of his legs in small increments. First the great toes were amputated then his fore-foot. Next came off the left leg from above the knee and a few months later the right just below the knee joint. Now he is dying, surrounded by at least twelve family members in the tiny cubicle among ticking, flashing, beeping and hissing instruments. The remaining thirty or so relatives chat in the waiting room, expecting to take turns to visit Willie.

Old Willie's granddaughter is a twenty-year-old single mom of three toddlers. She is the only one who asks the vascular surgeon to step outside for further questioning. He agreeably turns to leave but barely takes four steps when the woman promptly propositions him. He is caught off guard, cannot think to utter a single word. He went to school and trained for a combined twenty-five years and now he acts as a carp on a hook. His mouth agape, his eyes wide open and stare, and all he can do is squeeze a squeaky "Oh, no" out of his throat as he runs away. Of course, the girl and those of us in hearing distance, all laugh. She returns to Grandpa Willie and we rush to tell the story under the biggest secrecy to anyone who would listen.

Just then Mr. Johnston shuffles by as he does every afternoon. He faithfully visits his bride of sixty-two years since her surgery. She is always agitated before his arrival but he can calm her down. Whether it is his presence or the single gardenia floating in a plastic cup, who knows? When she gets progressively drowsy and finally falls asleep, he leaves for home.

Only after he is gone we discover his routine of sneaking into the hospital six ounces of vodka instead of water in the cup. By then the gardenia is tossed aside and wilted, Mrs. Johnston happily sleeps, and we all shake our heads in disbelief at the old man fooling us for a whole week.

When you think your doctor sees his patient only as another assignment he needs to complete in time, or as another disease he needs to diagnose, or as another person in his weakest moment somewhat pitiful and sometimes funny, think again. Look at his tired face from staying awake for the last twenty-six hours without hope to end his work soon. Look at his eyes filling with tears as he hugs a new widow and comforts the crying family. Look at his beaten down, bent back as he drags himself away from a dying patient and realizes how bad he feels to lose a fight for someone's life. Then you would know he tried his best, fought a fierce fight, waged his war, and learned to suffer an ultimate loss. Then you would understand and appreciate his smile and laughter with the patients and never about them, and you would smile and laugh in response readily with him if you ever find yourself in a hospital bed under his care.

Because you see, in a hospital a patient is not like you and me. But the doctors are.

19

*Oh what a tangled web we weave when
at first we start to deceive.*

———

Walter Scott

Dr. Ramsey's office was closed. The last patient left and his recently hired nurse was finishing her closing few tasks.

"Here is Marsha Redcliff's chart you asked for Doctor," she placed a red folder on his desk. "Is there anything else you need?"

He opened the folder and as he glanced at his visit note, asked her, "How did Dr. Redcliff talk with you? Did she complain to you of anything?"

"Marsha? Only her cough, nothing else. But I understand she always complained of that. It was not new. Why?"

"Just wondered. You were right. Her chronic complaints became quite boring and tiring to hear," he readily agreed.

"Didn't any of her medications work for her? How come? I know she refused the inhalers, but the others, like the cough syrup, should have made some difference, I would think. You know, she claimed none of the prescribed medications and treatments helped."

"Of course they didn't, how could they? She was

non-compliant. She didn't take them. God, she was frustrating." Dr. Ramsey searched the nurse's face as he talked.

"Don't worry, Doctor. Fortunately, nothing serious was going on; otherwise she would not look so healthy and well. Don't worry, I say. She worked full time, had a busy life, if anything was fatally wrong with her, she would have stopped working, I say." The nurse sounded confident. "What could be wrong with her? A nagging cough? Everyone has something to complain about. If that's all she's got, she has no problems, I say," she finished her assessment.

"I hope so, but you know how it is. If anything went wrong it would fall back on me because I did not treat her properly. Or some other similar claims."

"Why? Did she complain to you? She did not say a word to me when she left. True, she was awfully quiet, she did not even respond when I tried to set up a follow up visit for her. Did she stop coming here? You probably should have refused her care for non-compliance long ago, I say. That's legal, you know. My husband was let go by his doctor for the same reason, so I know it."

"No, I couldn't do that to a colleague, besides, she might badmouth me in the hospital. You know how it is. But I am glad you also saw how exasperating she was. What disturbs me more is that she did not talk to you. It's just not right to treat people like that, thinking they are on the lower level, beneath her. Come to think of it, maybe she considered herself being more than you or superior to you because she was a doctor and you are only a nurse," he probed.

"It never occurred to me before, but now as you mentioned it, perhaps that was on her mind. Too bad, I used to like her."

"Used to?" Dr. Ramsey repeated her.

"Yes. If she thinks she is better than a nurse then why should I break my back to like her? It just shows you. You never know how people can turn on you, I say. Not every doctor is like that, you certainly are not. You talk so nicely to everyone in the office, you are the nicest man, I say," she glanced at her watch then quickly added, "My, I am just chatting here and my kid probably is waiting for me to be picked up at school. Sorry doctor, I must run. See you in the morning."

Dr. Ramsey relaxed in his comfortable chair. He knew he could rely on his office nurse. She would not go against him. Should Dr. Redcliff ever complain about her missed diagnosis, he was certain this nurse would come to his defense.

He started to write an addendum on the bottom of the visit record, but as he turned the page a yellow sticky note caught him off guard, "Copies of record given to patient". The note was dated and initialed by his receptionist.

Dr. Ramsey just stared at the note and then re-read his addendum. If he was annoyed by Marsha's action, then he was infuriated by his own delay of not revoking the chart in time. Now it was too late, the Xerox copies printed the date and time on each page proving when the copy was made. There was no way he could add or modify his previous dictation.

His private phone rang. He picked it up though he knew well it was his wife insisting him to get out and be on his way home. She already called on the office phone only to discover it was turned over to the answering service. He had no excuse or reason to just sit there alone. And he better be alone if he knew what was good for him, she added. After assuring her that he was getting in the car in the next couple of minutes and was heading directly home, he pacified her enough to hang up.

He furiously began to blacken out his handwriting then thought it might still be detectable if anyone went to extremes to decipher the note beneath all the ink. One never knows, he had better play it safe. After a slight hesitation he picked up a long pair of shears and simply cut off the bottom of the page.

20

I see God in every human being.

———

Mother Teresa of Calcutta

The last days before her surgery, Marsha worked as usual. She seemed preoccupied but in a busy hospital everyone had enough to handle without too much spare time to analyze a coworker.

The Doctor's Lounge buzzed with the gossip of Dr. Marshall's divorce.

"Can you believe it? Getting a divorce and praying like a zealot before each surgery just don't go well together." Dr. Pribus approached Marsha.

"Maybe he was praying for his fraying marriage. Who knows? Furthermore, who cares?" Marsha asked.

"Of course being the Chairman of Surgery gets him respect, but I wonder if he will get the same respect afterward," another doctor chimed in the discussion.

"I think he is a genuinely nice man and regardless of what's going on in his life, nothing changed in his character," Hilda, with an unpronounceable German name remarked. She was an internist on an exchange program, working at Saint Cecilia for a year.

"You are wrong, this directly relates to his character.

On the surface he is religious, but underneath not so much if he ditches his wife."

"I hope his wife would get him for whatever he had, because he surely deserved it," an older female doctor added.

"I have heard him praying in the OR often. He always asked for a divine intervention and guidance so as not to make a mistake and be successful when he performed any surgeries." The surgical fellow was an authority because he worked shoulder to shoulder with Dr. Marshall.

"Well, he is not the only one who prays for help," interjected one of the diners. "General George Patton had pages and pages written in his diary about seeking God's help during his siege of the French city of Bastogne. He even prayed on Christmas Eve in a chapel for getting four days of good weather so his planes could fly and his tanks could roll. In exchange he offered God to send the Germans to their Valhalla, and end World War II." Everyone suspected for a while that he was a history buff, but the specific and detailed references he made left no doubt in their mind.

"Then it is the more preposterous to hear that he was filing for a divorce," concluded the gastroenterologist.

"Hey, Dr. Goldfinger, you should stick to your field, no pun intended," chuckled Marsha, "You are an expert in the lower end of the gut, not in marriage. If I recall correctly, you are not even married. Wait until you experience the earthly Paradise first!" Marsha laughed.

"C'mon, Dr. Spicy, leave him alone. He may work in crap, but it's his bread-and-butter!" laughed the anesthesiologist.

"Says who? It's coming from a gas-passer!" The gastroenterologist retorted.

"Well, we don't use gas anymore," the anesthesiologist

started to defend himself but his words were lost in the general laughter.

When Dr. Pribus disclosed the news to Marsha, she was just as surprised as he was in the beginning. Marsha met Noreen Marshall at a ballet performance about a year ago. She remembered that Noreen was much younger than Dr. Marshall; she must have been his second wife. The young woman had very little make up on and looked fresh and pretty. She liked her. Too bad she could not talk to her; they left earlier than she did. She saw Dr. Marshall tightly holding Noreen as he escorted his wife out of the theater. His left hand was on the back of her neck as if guiding her and he crossed himself to hang onto her arm with his right hand. His strange demeanor gave Marsha a very uncomfortable feeling. Maybe Dr. Marshall was a control freak and dominated her. Maybe he was not a totally holy man. The memories came back with vivid colors but she kept mum about her experience.

She asked, "So who is the new woman?"

The hospitalist looked at her in astonishment. "What do you mean, a new woman? I don't believe he has anyone."

"No man is leaving a wife without having a sure place to go." She replied flatly.

"I think he might be the exception. I haven't heard a thing about anyone else. I guess, they just grew apart."

"We'll see," replied Marsha shortly.

Another anesthesiologist softly laughed at the next table. "It's none of my business, but couldn't help to overhear your discussion. You are Dr. Redcliff who they call Dr. Spicy, right? I have heard about you. You are one-hundred percent right, Dr. Marshall has somewhere to go. I cannot name names, but if you check the list of the OR nurses you might find someone interesting there. A young and very attractive someone."

"See?" Asked Marsha victoriously. "Men are quite predictable."

The subject soon changed from Dr. Marshall to Dr. Khalid the cardiologist. His affair with his office nurse was an open secret for a long time. The smoldering fire gained strength when it became obvious that both his wife and girlfriend were pregnant. The two babies were delivered three weeks apart to the amazement and much talk of the community. Dr. Khalid's wife had been hospitalized at UH, but his girlfriend further stunned everyone by remaining at the local hospital. This daring step burst the glowing ambers of gossip into roaring flames. At long last Dr. Khalid had to decide what to do. At the end he divorced his wife and married his live-in girlfriend.

Interestingly, before the marriage Dr. Khalid was the talk of the town, but after he settled down, he was one of the boringly married men. No one bothered with him any further. His life was a sensational, titillating, secret drama before, and after his marriage it became an open book which no one wanted to read.

Marsha got up to leave. What difference did it make to her if Marshall divorced his wife for a nurse or if Khalid settled with his new family? Her life was not affected, it remained unchanged. She still had the lung cancer, and still had to face a major surgery soon. Before she could check into the hospital for the operation she had to finish seeing her patients and sign them over to her colleague. She had no time to chat today.

She stopped in the ER to evaluate a new case with fever and back ache. That's all I need today, thought Marsha, I already have a case of meningitis in ICU and I don't need a second one. The feverish old man was transferred from a nursing home the day before but there was no bed available so he stayed in the ER on the stretcher. So far neither the ER doctor nor the hospitalist had a diagnosis.

"I guess I would have a back ache too, laying on a gurney for two days," mumbled Marsha half audibly.

"Are you the urologist?" inquired the man on the stretcher.

"Nope, I am the neurologist. An almost urologist, but first you have to add an 'n' and an 'e' to the word 'urologist'."

"A neurologist?" He was obviously not told of the pending evaluation. "What do you do?"

"Oh, it's like being a urologist, except I work upstairs and not in the South Pole," joked Marsha. "Let me examine you."

The man was lucid enough to warn her, "Unless you have your galoshes on, don't press on my bladder".

She smiled, "I would not dare to Mr. Hawks. Besides I have my high heels on today." She finished the examination by turning him over only to discover a small group of blisters near his tailbone. "But at least I know what's wrong with you. Have you had chickenpox as a child?"

"Long, long ago my lady," came the response.

"Well, you have the same virus but now it's on your butt only. I'll give you some medications and it will go away. Just be careful, it is infectious."

"If any woman comes close enough to catch it then she deserves it," he cackled.

Marsha casually asked the ER physician, "You certainly detected the shingles when you examined him, didn't you? If you had pulled off his briefs you wouldn't have missed the blisters." The man just stared at her. It was obvious he did not, because he only ordered a urine test and a chest X-ray searching for a possible infection elsewhere.

As she left the ER she passed an open door and peaked in the room to see her next patient. The overweight man sat in his bed, in front of him a McDonald's double decker and a large order of cheesy fries. In his left hand he held a tall paper cup of Coke while he stuffed his mouth with the food from the greasy wrapper.

Marsha stepped into the room and cheerfully asked the man, "Is that what I ordered for your meal?"

He defiantly replied, "No, but I can't eat the hospital food. It tastes like crap."

"Funny you say that. I eat the same hospital food every day and did not die yet. Of course I never tasted crap, so I would not know how crap tasted to compare them." Marsha retorted. "Seriously, you just had your third mini-stroke, have sky-high blood pressure and cholesterol, and you eat fast food. Do you know how much salt and fat is in this meal? And your diabetes will not thank you for the bun, the fries, and the Coke, either."

"What do you want me to do?" Asked the man and was hesitant to grab another handful of fries. The melted yellow cheese dripped from between his fingers and curled toward his wrist.

"Well, I devoted years to learn things so I can teach you what to do. I spent yesterday at least an hour with you explaining what you need to change. The way I see it you have two choices: you can both learn from me and hopefully live longer or you don't follow the recommendations and pay for my tuition. Because you will return with a stroke. And you might not be so lucky next time. It's up to you."

As she left the room she bumped into the physical therapist. He was armed with a folded walker and a safety belt, ready to attack the same man.

"Hey Dr. Redcliff, did you hear the four phases of overweight?" He asked.

"By size, weight or by BMI? I know only these three," replied Marsha.

"Neither, it's a joke. The four phases are overweight, obese, morbidly obese, and Oh my God!" Came the laughing response.

"Oh that," said Marsha, "In that case you better exercise this guy, because he is somewhere between the third and fourth stage. If he continues with the cheesy fry, it soon will be a full OMG!""

Next she visited the feistiest ninety-three year old woman she has ever encountered. Ruby Maldonado barely spoke English but she was more animated than Sarah Bernhardt. Her face told the whole world what she thought and what she felt. Funny, there were people who wore their emotions like their clothes, ready to be seen by everyone, decided Marsha. Parting she patted the old woman's hand but Ruby Maldonado grabbed her and pulled her down and before Marsha realized, she planted a huge kiss on her face.

In ICU she had three seriously ill patients. The older man's spinal fluid came back positive for West Nile Virus caused meningitis. He had high fever and wildly thrashed around in his bed, not knowing where he was or what he was saying. His antiviral medications continuously dripped into his veins and Marsha hoped they were able to combat the invisible army which invaded his brain and hijacked his mind.

The younger man was an illegal immigrant. He had no insurance and no means to pay for any of his medical care. His admitting diagnosis was new onset seizures but his brain images showed several round lesions with a central brighter dot. Marsha realized she was looking at the classic presentation of neurocysticercosis. She explained the big word in easily understood terms to Mr. Gonzales.

"Do you eat pork? How do you make it? I am interested in your cooking," she started.

"Si, Señora Doctora." Mr. Gonzales rapidly talked for a long time. Marsha helplessly waited for the translation. She was always amazed at her Hispanic patients as they forever used to reply to simple questions with lengthy answers. At times when she lost patience and asked the interpreter what was said in the last five minutes, the answer inevitably was a "He said 'No'."

Finally the truth was revealed: Mr. Gonzales heard Americans ate beef steak while bloody red. Well, beef steak was hard to come by in the power stricken Yucatan peninsula, but pork was readily available in Mexico. Mr. Gonzales decided to eat pork bloody red also. The infected meat harbored the larva which traveled along the highways of his blood vessels and then lodged in his brain. He faced long-term medication treatment with the added possible lifelong anti-seizure medications. The interpreter explained to him that he had to cook his pork until it was soft enough to melt in his mouth, until he could cut it without a knife. He absolutely could not eat pork with blood running or even while pink in the center. Marsha was not convinced Mr. Gonzales agreed with her instructions. She knew several more discussions were needed before he could be convinced of his doctor's truth.

Her third patient had a sad history. He worked as a field engineer when he first twisted his ankle. This weakness progressed to buckling his knee which occasionally resulted in a fall. He was treated for arthritis, neuropathy, and various obscure rheumatoid diseases before an electromyogram and nerve conduction study diagnosed him with Lou Gehrig disease. That was almost four years ago. He gradually lost control over every muscle of his body, only his eyes moved freely at will. He was tube fed and on a ventilator. Marsha convinced the social workers to paint a long strip of large letters of the alphabet which she posted on the wall, across from Mr. Donlevy. By focusing his eyes on the appropriate letter ahead of him, he could spell out words and slowly communicate with the nurses and his rare visitors.

After finishing with her ICU patients, she was asked to write a peripheral neuropathy medication prescription for Kira, the med-surg nurse. As soon as she handed her the prescription, Kira revealed she finally got insurance and Marsha didn't have to help her out anymore.

"I will never forget you lending a hand. Thanks so much," she gushed, but Marsha only asked her to keep it between them. She didn't want to encounter more of these so-called curb-side consultations.

"Hi Marsha, I haven't seen you all week, where were you hiding?" Hearing the cheerful voice of Dr. Johnson, she gladly stopped to wait for him. When he caught up with her, they continued walking together.

"Don't tell me you missed me," Marsha teased him.

"I sure did. I was thinking of you as soon as I laid eyes on the Buckingham Palace. Actually, I wondered if you could be there having a spot of tea with Betty." His British accent was suddenly exaggerated to almost being a parody.

"Betty? Betty who?" Marsha wondered.

"The Queen, silly. I was joking."

"Aw, I invited her here but she didn't show up," Marsha continued the light weight bantering then asked with genuine interest, "What's new? Any new discoveries? Didn't you just return from London? How did it go?" Marsha was curious. For the previous six months all she heard from Dr. Johnson was his exploration of the English ancestors. He delved into seeking the distant past as if his present existence depended on it and frequently updated Marsha with his findings.

"Uh, don't ask. I don't want to talk about it. All I can tell you is, I am done with the research of my family tree, for sure."

"How come? Didn't you discover some aristocrat relative living in a giant castle or something like that there? Hey, you could do all of us a favor and take the dragon-lady Sarah to guard your castle. Seriously, didn't you say you found a distant cousin in London?"

"Distant cousin all right," Frank Johnson crunched up his face, "He was a derelict. A homeless drunk," he lowered his voice, "You know in my whole life I believed that all men are our brothers, but at times like this it's awful hard to believe it. No, that pickled old goat was not someone I would brag about, for sure."

"Oh-oh, that was unexpected, I guess. But since you traveled that far, did you find out anything else? Like other relatives, dead or alive, anything?" Marsha pressed further.

"I tell you, but only you and don't you dare speak about it to anyone. Promise? I went to the city archives and the church registry. I traced back my family to the seventeen-hundreds. All the way to my ancestor, Francis R. Johnson."

"Wow, that's spectacular, Frank."

"Hold it. It's not so wonderful. He was hung by the neck for stealing a horse."

Caught off guard, she stopped in her stride and turned to face him. Elegant, educated, tall, and slim Dr. Johnson, thought to be the descendant of old English nobility, was in reality the descendant of a horse thief? She busted out laughing.

"Frank, it could have only happened to you, I swear,"

she barely was able to get out the words. "So what's next?"

"Nothing. Nothing is next. I am done with digging for my ancestors. Let them rest. And don't you ever tease me with them or I will never talk to you again!" He warned her playfully.

Marsha imitated a circus horse, hitting her foot to the ground, "One clunk is for 'yes', I will not tease you, ever." She stepped into the elevator. Although the door blocked Dr. Johnson from her view, she kept laughing all the way down to the second floor.

"Dr. Redcliff, could you see room 245? I think he is on his way out. He wanted to talk to you." The charge nurse called her from the nurses' station.

"Sure, I will go right away."

"Oh and 211 was discharged earlier but left this envelope for you."

Marsha opened the unsealed envelope only to find a pretty card. She read it as she slowly walked and smiled, remembering the visiting, old, black lady from Alabama. The handwriting revealed a hand not used to a pencil, but the deliberately drawn individual letters obviously were dictated from her heart: "Girlie: You are the bee's knees with personality and what a personality! Thank you and God bless!"

"You're welcome. It is I who should thank you," She whispered. "Gosh, I haven't been called a 'girlie' since Noah and the Great Flood!"

Mr. Anthony Tanner's room was silent; obviously no one wanted to disturb him. The old man resting in the bed barely breathed. Marsha stood by his bedside quietly watching his chest rise and fall, realizing the light of his life barely flickered. When he opened his eyes he looked at Marsha and whispered in a weak voice, "Thank you for coming. It's not nice to go home alone. Would you hold my hand?"

He seemed to visibly relax as soon as Marsha's warm hand wrapped around his arthritic, deformed fingers. Perhaps the touch or perhaps the last flare up of his energy gave him the strength to whisper a few more words.

"You were kind to me, you did not mind touching me. I know it must be hard, even disgusting sometimes to touch an old man's warped body. Once long ago ... I was young ... and even handsome, not like I am now." After a long pause he added, "You would have liked me then."

Marsha squeezed the cold, waxy fingers a bit harder and tried to transfer some of her own warmth into his hand.

"You see, I was created to the likeness of the Creator. Whether I was young and healthy or old and ill, this remained the same... This is the secret you must remember always... It might be hard for you at times, but when you face a particularly revolting patient you just close your eyes and say to yourself 'I touch the face of God when I touch you'. You'll see, it makes your work so much easier."

With his pale and cold fingers he hung onto Marsha's warm hand, his last earthly contact, and then haltingly whispered, "We all have to end one day. It matters not who you are, what you do, what you have. The rich and the poor, the tall and the short, men or women in all colors and creed, they all have to come to an end one day... But when it's the home run, when you see the end, all of a sudden it becomes effortless... Everything is easier at the end."

He raised his head up from the pillow, his old eyes suddenly sparkled with surprise and joy and he happily cried out, "Thank you for coming. I knew you would be with me, you will not abandon me. Go ahead and I will follow you." Marsha turned around but saw no one in the room. Yet, it was clear, an expected and loved person welcomed the old man and he joyfully went along with his invisible guide.

A vicious coughing spell stopped his talk. His eyes opened wide in fear as he gasped for air. He raised his upper body off the bed in terror. Marsha increased the oxygen level to maximum but he fell back to his pillow and was gone. His cornflower blue eyes halfway open, still stared at Marsha.

She softly closed his eyes and quickly drew an almost imperceptible cross on his forehead. Her favorite patient Anthony Tanner, the old pastor, went home. He was at rest.

21

I am prepared for the worst, but hope for the best.

Benjamin Disraeli

After the initial jolt of cancer diagnosis wore off, Marsha felt fully alert, almost vigilant, in every moment and every moment she downright lived. But things were not the same any more. Looking at her precious "House of Sunshine", she no longer had the usual gratifying feeling; instead she burst out in a bitter disappointment, "What for? What difference does it make? It has no value, no meaning, none at all." She felt nothing but emptiness. She lost what she valued before; everything became a useless material article. The world itself lost its vibrant colors and became hollow. She realized all her work, her efforts, her dreams, her plans were in vain. "Vanity of vanities, all is vanity."

She critically evaluated every comment and started to watch carefully everyone she contacted. She no longer missed the slightest, unrelated or insignificant remark, no further ignored what she found unpleasant or disagreeable. Her greatest transformation came with no longer offering her blind trust to anyone, unearned, not even if he was a colleague or another doctor. Especially not for another doctor.

She was preparing for the worst while hoping for a miracle. One evening as she put in order her Health Care Surrogate form and Last Will she was confronted with the possibility of a pending funeral and related expenses. She decided her ashes should be buried in the grave of her parents. After all she started her life with them when they gave her birth; it was right to finish it between them also. Because she did not want to burden her sons, the following day she made arrangement for her cremation and burial.

Once all preparations were in order and completed, she put on the finishing touch by compiling a phone list. Her children should not find difficult to notify relatives and friends of the outcome. She labeled the various keys for easy identification and organized her personal files, again trying to help them.

The clothes and shoes in the drawers and closets were arranged by colors or neatly stored. Even the slightest discoloration ended them in a bag to be donated to the Salvation Army. It was unbelievable how much junk she accumulated. She finally realized that whenever she was to leave this earth she was not going to take a single thing. Coffins did not come with a U-Haul. Everyone was to leave as arrived: naked and alone.

"Marsha, your problem is you worry about people's opinions," her friend Maggie concluded. "If you expect to die, at least realize if anyone thought of Marsha Redcliff negatively you wouldn't know it. If your house was not in perfect order, who cares? You wouldn't hear the remarks. As a matter of fact I hope you would be so busy having fun and excitement on the last day of your life that your house would be left in total disarray. So why break your back? It's futile to leave everything picture perfect. Instead, you should enjoy the day."

Debbie and Maggie helped her choose new nightgowns and robes for the hospital stay. Neither could explain Marsha's sudden extravagant shopping. Every item was either Oscar de la Renta or Ralph Lauren. As a last purchase she added a large bottle of Bvalgari perfume to her bag. At last Marsha realized that money no longer mattered and savings were pointless. In any case, this way no one should say she didn't go in style.

During dinner the discussion turned to a wish-list: Debbie wanted enough money to spoil her grandchildren more and Maggie wanted to return to Italy.

Marsha admitted, "I always wanted to visit Bora Bora. I imagine this enchanted island exactly as the travel posters pictured. Maybe it is not quite as pristine or gorgeous in real life but it sure would be nice to see it one day!"

"Why don't you go then?" Debbie asked her, but Maggie quickly added, "You should go if you want it so much. It's not that expensive, you can afford it."

"What's the use of dreaming about something and letting the years slide by without fulfilling any part of a dream?" Debbie offered a down-to-earth solution, "When you recover from surgery, you should go. It's settled then, let's drink to that."

Of course there were many evenings when she was not as composed as she appeared in public and there were many nights when she could not sleep. Alone and in the safety of her home she could cry freely.

She felt sad over the loss of everything she was, she had, or she had known. She mourned her failing body, her unfulfilled dreams, losing her little world. Most of all she feared not knowing where she would go and what would become of her. If this was not enough to dismay her, the unknown and the insecure future clutched at her chest with an ice-cold, creeping sensation.

She instantly teared up when looking at something beautiful such as a new flower opening in her garden, seeing the baby mockingbirds in the nest in her grape arbor, or watching the reflection of sunrise on the lake. She sadly thought that all these would remain here to be admired long after she was gone.

When she could not sleep, she looked at the sky for hours. Her younger son sent her a map of the skies and now she looked to identify the constellations by the phosphorescent picture of heavenly bodies. How gorgeous this secret, mystic world seemed!

She wondered if there was life in any form in the vast universe. There had to be. It was logical that everything seemed predestined in life, perfectly planned in the human body and the world. It was unfathomable that death annihilated what was there before. Maybe this new life would not be in the form that she could imagine with her current limited understanding. Perhaps it would occur in some other dimension – in a different shape, yet in some way salvaging something from this mortal body. Maybe only the thoughts, energy, emotion and above all, love survived and stepped over the decay. It was impossible that all would fade into zero and cease to exist forever. Surely there was a little shelter in the infinite universe for saving whatever outlived an earthly life.

When she finally fell into an exhausted, dreamless sleep, she did it with the sad but comforting thought that soon she would know it. In her newly gained calmness, she imagined that seeing all from Heaven everything would look incomparably more beautiful.

The weekend prior to the fast-approaching surgery her older, then two days later the younger child arrived. Knowing they would be under stress, Marsha prepared a list of everything she could think of, everything that needed to be conveyed to them. She gave a copy of her Last Will to each and showed them where she kept her finances, her bills, and the accounts to cover the expenses. She pointed out to them the few pieces she inherited from her parents and grandparents, asking them to save those for their children. The rest of her household with all its material value, lost its importance.

The last night before she had to show up in the hospital, she reviewed her life in her mind and was satisfied that she had accomplished everything she wanted. She became a physician. True, in order to become one she had to jump through flaming hoops like a trained tiger in a circus but in the end, she did it. She wrote and published three books, got awards for one and applause for the others. She gathered great friends from every stage of her life and kept their friendship throughout the years. She helped whoever she could, often without being asked. When she saw the need, she just did it. She really did not have any big dreams or desires left unfulfilled. She had a good life.

She reached closure in her mind. She arranged everything the best way she could. From now on it was up to her children to carry on with life. She gave them a solid, straight foundation and now it was up to them to build a wall on it. She hoped they would raise a sturdy house on this groundwork, one that would withstand the storms of life. She was passing on the baton. She was convinced she placed it into good and strong hands. Her conscience was clear and she was at peace.

22

*Mind control is built on lies and manipulation
of attachment needs.*

———

Valerie Sinason

Since Marsha Redcliff got a leave of absence, Dr. Pacheco took care of all neurology patients. Between the innumerable false ER alerts, the daily acute strokes, and the inpatients, she constantly was running in between the various departments. Dr. Ferguson jokingly called her a pendulum.

Periodically she asked for help to no avail. None of the neurologists came to her rescue. Dr. Marlene was the head of the group and claimed his extra administrative duties took up most of his time. The other two were useless as far as Pacheco could see. One functioned better on the golf course than in the office, and the other was simply too lazy to do anything beyond the required minimum.

The hospital administration recognized the validity of her pleas but either did not want or did not care to shell out more money for the neurology coverage. Aside from getting verbal support and projected help in the near future, everything remained the same. Recognizing her hard work, at the end of the year the hospital awarded Dr.

Pacheco the prestigious I Care Award for Accountability. She was selected from three-hundred-sixty physicians to receive the honor. In the end, the engraved crystal disk served as a nice desk decoration. The award was not accompanied by either a single penny or an hour of help in her work.

Of course, behind the scenes the neurology group and the hospital administration kept fighting for money and better coverage. Since both held the other accountable and claimed no ownership over the results, it was hopeless to expect any change.

For some ridiculous reason, Sarah predictably called Dr. Pacheco a couple of times each day, but eventually she learned not to answer her phone. Instead, at the end of the day she returned all her calls at once which usually accumulated to nothing else but harassment. Once seeing the caller ID, a few of the nurses who could not stand Sarah, volunteered to pick up the phone on her behalf. Invariably they stated "The doctor was with a patient and could not be disturbed because she was in the midst of a procedure." They promised to relay the message to her and hung up the phone. After one of these phone calls an annoyed nurse angrily added "Lady, you really should park your broom elsewhere." But the continuing daily calls didn't indicate that Sarah got the message.

A few times she truly should not have been disturbed with Sarah's nonsensical office trouble because she attended emergencies in both the ER and on the floors. The last shake-up occurred when they had to break dawn the staff bathroom door because it remained locked for a long time. They could not get any response after a loud crash was heard from within. When finally the burly maintenance man forced the door open they found Krista Jones, RN on the floor. Her right hand gripped a syringe, her left forearm had a tourniquet tied on and the needle was still embedded in her vein. No matter how they tried to revive her, Krista was dead from a heroin overdose.

She happened to be a recently hired nurse and no one really befriended her, yet. Although everyone was shocked, not a loud word was said about the incident. It was simply acknowledged, whispered about repeatedly among themselves, and then swept under the rug. Out of sight, it was never mentioned again. It soon faded as a black day in the life in the hospital.

Dr. Jane Pacheco had her own problems. For two years she felt like she was being used as a pawn in the chess game played by Dr. Marlene and the hospital administrator. She was careful not to stir the pot and took every assignment cheerfully. She loved her profession and preferred hospital care to outpatient office, she enjoyed her job.

She repeatedly said "I love my work so much that it's almost a sin to get paid for it."

Dr. Marlene responded with an "OK, then we shouldn't issue your next check," and they laughed. Dr. Pacheco gave an uncomfortable chuckle and Dr. Marlene cackled while pondering on the possibility.

In the beginning Dr. Marlene ordered the office manager to place a whole page announcement in the newspaper of a new neurologist joining the group. Although it increased business, it also attracted an unwanted response. One day Dr. Pacheco received an envelope addressed to her. The return address was the local Federal Prison, followed by a chain of numbers, most likely the prisoner's ID. The sender claimed himself to be her Tarzan ("You are Jane, aren't you?") and projected a happy reunion as soon as he got paroled. At the end of the letter he added the heartfelt poem he wrote to her:

"With your angelic face,
Heaven is the place
Where you should be,
But you should die
If you don't hear my cry,
Then I could love you forever."

Dr. Pacheco was frightened. The felon knew her work place and the hospital was open to all visitors. Her personal information and picture were spread on the newspaper page. If he was to be paroled he could come to the hospital and if angered could gun her down. It happened in other health care facilities. It could occur here, too.

She complained to Dr. Marlene, "See, this is the reason why I objected to this big advertisement. I understand it was good for your business but it resulted in me being targeted and I am scared. My address and phone number are public knowledge and he can recognize me by the picture. He can get to me either here or at my apartment. What do you say to that?"

"Maybe we should invest in a good life insurance for you," replied Dr. Marlene.

"If you were joking it was rather ill placed, don't you think? Would you say the same if it was your wife or teenage daughter?"

"My wife yes, for my daughter, no," her boss continued to jest.

Dr. Pacheco left him without response. What was there to say? Dr. Marlene neither understood nor protected her. He also refused to claim any ownership in creating the dangerous development.

Next she turned to the head of the hospital security. The ex-policeman took her concern very seriously and promised to contact the prison where the letter originated from and accidentally missed inspection. Dr. Jane Pacheco nervously watched every face she came in contact with ever since she received the threatening letter. She expected to be attacked at any moment and feared the worst, but nothing happened. Eventually, the panic dissipated but the resentment toward Dr. Marlene remained in her.

The days rolled by; some relatively quiet but most peppered with unreasonable requests and outright agitation. When she had enough of the daily harassment, she resigned. Almost immediately, she regretted submitting her letter of resignation because her teenage son was unexpectedly placed in a Rehab Center which cost almost as much as her monthly salary. She needed her job badly; yet, she could not tell anyone what her true reasons were behind the sudden change of her mind. She carefully backtracked by citing her loyalty to the group, enjoyment of her hospital position, and love for the patients. No one believed her reasoning but Dr. Marlene happily accepted her decision.

By sheer luck the danger resolved spontaneously and the contract to provide hospital coverage continued uninterrupted. It was an especially critical time because Dr. Redcliff was on leave of absence. If Dr. Pacheco left, then the three neurologists had to divide the hospital work among themselves until they found a replacement.

The initial celebration and good will soon soured. Realizing Dr. Pacheco was forced to remain in the job and for some reason could not leave; she became their property to be abused. If she thought she had been harassed before, now she learned that bullying had no limits. Provocation, pestering, annoyance, and aggravation all had to be taken with a smile if she wanted to pay for her son's rehabilitation. Although she got a small increase in her salary she felt every dollar was smeared by her blood. The saying "Mothers can tolerate the gravest injustice for their children" was true.

The only benefit of her recent action surprisingly came from the hospital administration. They even petitioned the neurology group to release Dr. Pacheco from her contract so the hospital could hire her directly. After prolonged negotiations the proposed project was nixed by Dr. Marlene citing legal responsibilities and limitations.

Mr. Lawler bitterly registered the group's rejection and remarked, "Marlene acts like an old, toothless dog. He cannot chew the bone any more, but God forbid to let a younger dog to have it."

The month after Dr. Pacheco's son was released from the rehab hospital, she left the group without regrets. She loathed the three neurologists who loaned her to the hospital but always claimed to be the happiest when she worked with the Cecilia Beach staff and took care of their patients.

23

Although the world is full of suffering,
It is also full of the overcoming of it.

Helen Keller

Andy Redcliff woke his mother up at an ungodly four in the morning then drove her to the hospital. Marsha gave him directions on the road and what to eat when he got home. He looked at her sideways without any comments. Clearly, he did not enjoy her overabundance of motherly love.

"I know I better stop," she started, "you are thirty-three, and have two kids of your own, who am I kidding? You are surely able to take care of yourself without my help. But I had been a mother for over thirty-six years now and by now I got used to the part. You do understand that I'm not able to turn the motherly role off as if it were a switch?"

A few moments later she added, "You know, to worry is a God-given duty of every mother."

He jokingly retorted, "Yep, and at times yours is in overdrive. I know it's genetically stapled, especially today. I know, it's OK."

After she was wheeled into the pre-op room, Andy hugged her tight for a long time. His face was strained and serious. "I will be here, I will not leave for a minute. You will never be alone, I will be with you." Marsha knew he would. Andy was always loving, reliable, and steadfast even as a child and remained the same as an adult. His words echoed in her mind and she knew she would remember them as long as she lived.

Debbie arrived and was escorted to her bedside. She smiled encouragingly, "I will keep Andy's company, because he will need it. Maggie just called me; she was on her way and should arrive shortly. I saw Diana's car pulling in the parking lot, she should be here any moment. We'll make sure Andy is ok. Between the three of us he won't be bored, I can assure you."

Everything went on like clockwork and by the time Dr. Verdi greeted her, she was wrapped in a blue hospital gown and clear fluid infused in the veins of her arms.

"Are you ready? I am glad you remembered we had an early morning date," Dr. Verdi joked. "I met your son and promised him I would update him periodically so he wouldn't worry too much." He chatted with Marsha for a few more minutes before he left to scrub for surgery.

Dr. Verdi looked rested, even-tempered, positive, and pleasant. He radiated self-assurance and confidence. He meant security to Marsha.

Her spinal drip anesthesia needle was barely inserted in her upper spine when someone injected a quick acting sedative in her IV line. Her head became heavy, it was hard to focus and she could not concentrate. She felt rapidly sinking into a deep, warm, and dark void. Faintly she heard a voice calling from a distance, "Are you guys ready? C'mon, let's get going. Dr. Verdi is waiting."

Marsha didn't care, whatever happened there, it no longer concerned her. Her last conscious thought was, "Father, into your hands I command..." She could not complete the sentence. She fell asleep and didn't even know it.

⁓

Dr. Verdi felt tired. For three hours he leaned over the operating table, focusing on the open side of his patient as he adjusted the bright light burning above his head. Through the gaping wound he manipulated various instruments to probe, cut, seal, and remove pieces of tissue in order to get rid of the cancerous growth.

"One can never truly predict what will be found before the first cut is made," he said to no one in particular. It almost sounded as if he was talking to himself. "What's planned as a simple surgery may turn out to be a nightmare. Like this here."

His assistant on the opposite side of the sleeping patient looked questioningly at him above his mask, but remained silent.

"Just look at all these adhesions, they are horrendous. For the last three hours all we did was try to peel and separate the lining of the chest from the lung. It's incredible. What the heck is going on?" Dr. Verdi felt the frustration building up inside and he knew he had to take a break before it engulfed him completely. "Take over for ten minutes, would you? I have to stretch my back a bit; my shoulders are starting to cramp again."

On his way out he glanced at the anesthesiologist who comfortably leaned back on his chair at the head of the table with his feet propped up. He instantly assured the surgeon, "Take your time, she is doing fine. Her pressure is stable and she is visiting La-la land."

As soon as Dr. Verdi appeared in the waiting room door, the four people huddled in the corner jumped up and expectantly looked at him. First he patted Andy's shoulder and smiled at him, "Don't be frightened, everything is going well right on schedule. Just as planned." He then turned to Debbie and Maggie, "Ladies are you keeping him from worrying too much?" Looking at Diana, he seemed to be startled, "Don't I know you from ICU? You are a nurse in there, right? Are you girls all friends with Dr. Redcliff?" The three women simultaneously bobbed their heads in agreement.

"So, we opened up your mom's chest on the right side, about right here," and he indicated the cut on Andy's torso. "It's kind of difficult to get in deep yet, because she had so much adhesion there. You know, when things get stuck it's never a normal thing. It's such a tedious job, it takes time to separate them. I have to use the microscope to make infinitely tiny cuts otherwise I would nip or damage areas which would require extra reparation. Now we don't want that, do we?"

Andy hung onto his every word. "Mom OK though, isn't she?"

"Yes, she is. She is asleep and doesn't feel a thing. Of course she is safe. We are taking good care of her, don't worry. Her pressure and pulse are stable, and she gets fluids and lots of antibiotics so no chance to have an infection. If we had made a bigger cut in her like we used to do this for surgery decades ago, we probably would be finished by now. But with more work on my side, she will end up with a smaller scar and much less pain in the end. So bear with me and I promise to come back again to update you."

"Before you go back" Andy turned to him, "Could you tell about when you would expect it to be over?"

"Probably another two to three hours I would say. I will let you know when we get close to wrapping it up."

He went back to the operating room, and the three ladies hugged each other and Andy.

Dr. Verdi quickly gulped down his coffee, stretched his back to shake the burning pain out, and shrugged his shoulders to loosen the tight muscles. He entered the surgical suit to take over the tedious procedure again.

It was way after lunch time when the recovery room nurse called Andy's name and led him to Marsha's bedside. Dr. Verdi was just covering her up after adjusting her chest tubes as he checked the drainage. Andy began to feel faint, looking at his mother's ghostly white face, and the bloody fluid in the large container that drained from her chest.

"I thought you said the operation was on the right..." he said. "What are those two tubes on her left then?"

Dr. Verdi smiled, "Indeed, the surgery was on the right. That's where we worked. The left is where I put the two tubes in to drain the accumulating fluid or she would drown in her own secretions and blood."

"Oh, so she has both sides affected now."

"Yes, that's how it works. Once the drainage stops, the tubes come out. That's not permanent."

"Isn't it too uncomfortable for her being hurt on both sides? She could not turn to either side now."

"You would think, but we give her lots of pain medications, so she doesn't suffer. Trust me. She would not want to turn anyway now, even if she could. You can talk to her but don't expect her to remember anything afterward. She is just coming out of anesthesia."

"Thank you, Dr. Verdi, thanks for saving my mother. She is a good person. She deserves it." Andy's eyes filled with tears.

"Of course she is. She will be fine. I will come back later to see her but once she is stable, she goes to ICU. There are other doctors and specially trained nurses to take good care of her. But don't worry, I will keep a close eye on her. And, ah, yes, if you have any questions, just tell them to call me. Any time," he said and disappeared behind the double doors.

Finally, Dr. Verdi was ready to sit down and relax after six and a half-hour of concentration, straining his eyes under the special goggles, manipulating his fingers deftly and precisely to control his instruments. Suddenly it dawned on him he did not eat a bite all day, only had a paper cup of black coffee, and for the last eight hours had no time to go to the men's room, either.

Pain. Excruciating, searing pain, increasing with every breath whether inhaled or exhaled. Pain that prevents the slightest movement of any part of the body. Pain which responds poorly to medications though the drugs might immobilize the body and knock the mind out. Pain that was always present and even felt through the numbing effects of the analgesics.

In the first three days Marsha suffered agonizing pain. There were only fragments of these days embedded in her mind's eye with each mosaic colored by the overwhelming suffering. The individual slivers of memory remained disconnected and forever impossible to make a complete picture.

She opened her eyes to see Debbie's dark silhouette against a bright window. Another time she spotted her son, one leg across his other knee and his laptop in front of him. He looked up and seeing Marsha opening her eyes came to her bedside. By the time he had crossed the few steps between them, she lost contact with him again. Once she vaguely registered Diana's request for a pain pump and a second IV line for her so she did not have to wait for the pain medication until after her antibiotic was finished. At another time she heard Dr. Verdi's voice but was too groggy to respond him. Vaguely she thought she should not ignore him but she had neither the will nor the power to remain awake.

Andy changed the cool wet washcloth on her forehead to make her more comfortable when her fever spiked. She woke up to her son's soft, encouraging voice, "Mom, have a bit of Jell-O, it will feel good," as he tried to spoon-feed her but she was too tired to open her mouth. She could not swallow anyway. Her mouth and throat were on fire, a drop of water felt as if she tried to swallow razor blades.

A nurse offhandedly said, "Oh, it's nothing, it's just thrush. It always happens after we give massive antibiotics. They got changed anyway, because her bladder infection was not sensitive to them. Mention it to her doctor, maybe he would put her on some medication."

The following day her doctor detected a small pneumothorax on the chest X-ray, so the chest tubes had to remain in place longer. With the ongoing pneumonia, and everything else going wrong, she felt miserable. Each time she finally found a fraction of comfort by sliding down in the bed, two nurses pulled her up to the top. On the count of "one, two, three" her two torturers pulled her into proper position by grabbing her draw-sheet and jerking her aching body to previously unknown level of agony.

"Stay up in your bed. Why do you always have to slide down? Do you have rollers on your butt? You are not a good patient," they scolded her. She searched for a new sky-light in the ceiling for she was certain she made one when they yanked her into the position of a "good patient."

Andy stayed with her from early morning to late night and took care of her. She became the child and he became the parent. Marsha felt comforted, although the whole thing somehow felt wrong. These roles were not supposed to be reversed. Yet, she readily accepted his caring and sank into the love he showered on her.

Two young graduate nurses apparently took a liking in her. They were both very pretty and talkative. The taller of the two could have passed for a fashion model.

"How do you feel today? Is everything alright?" They smiled and kept chatting with her. Both pleasantly greeted Debbie and Andy, asking who was a relative and who was a visitor. Learning who Andy was, the taller nurse instantly set herself to discover about him as much as she could. The shorter nurse was more reserved but also seemed interested in him.

"So you are Dr. Redcliff's son," said the taller girl, "Do you live with her?"

"No, I live in California. I just came for her surgery," Andy replied.

"That was very nice of you. Good that you could take off from your job. What do you do?"

"I run an IT department, so I really can do everything on the computer from anywhere and while mom sleeps I work. My office is right in this corner," he smiled pointing to his chair under the window.

"That's great; your company must like you to let you do it. How about your family? You do have a family there, don't you?" The inquisition continued.

"My ex-wife took the kids for the week. No problem. My mom was the priority."

"Oh, so you are divorced!" It was impossible to miss the pleasant surprise in her voice. Then she cheerfully continued, "I just adore children! I am the favorite aunt to all my nieces and nephews. They are convinced I would make a far better mother than their own mom." The blonde girl sweetly smiled. She was sort of expecting a response from Andy but he leaned forward to turn off his laptop and his face was hidden.

The blonde nurse with the pony tail asked a lot more questions about California because she "always wanted to go there," she said. "I would consider moving there but would want to visit it first," she added. Andy remained quiet.

The two young nurses several times popped in Marsha's room every day just to ask her if she needed anything or if they could do something for her. They stayed a while to chat with Andy. Marsha was content with the thought that finally she impressed someone in this hospital by her personality or, if nothing else, by being a physician. She was slightly abashed to assume that she was the focus of their interest; after her handsome son left for Los Angeles neither of the two young nurses ever came back to visit her.

24

This above all; to thine own self be true.

William Shakespeare

Cecilia Beach Community Hospital was buzzing with the news of Dr. Redcliff's absence. Within days everyone knew that Dr. Redcliff underwent some sort of surgery at the University Hospital (UH), but no one was sure why or what was wrong with her. Her coworkers questioned each other in an attempt to gain more information before they spread their limited knowledge to others.

The Petri-dish, aka the Doctor's Lounge had no other topic at lunchtime but Marsha Redcliff's illness. Her substitute was first approached but she could not add anything new to the already murky data so the sympathetic and curious colleagues turned to Dr. Ramsey.

"You must have heard she went to the UH for surgery, didn't you? What happened, do you know?" One by one they questioned him.

Dr. Ramsey quietly answered them, "I cannot say anything, although I was her pulmonologist and treated her for the last three years. When you have a chronic cough, especially at her age, it's very ominous. And very sad. No matter what you do, eventually you reach the point when you cannot do any more. The poor thing, it's just awful. You understand me, I am sure." He left the prying man in total shock.

After that shrouded revelation, it didn't take much before the whole hospital knew Marsha Redcliff was dying. Three ICU nurses cornered Dr. Ramsey after the morning rounds. "Is it true that Dr. Redcliff is ill? We heard she had surgery and not doing well," stated Josè.

"Unfortunately, it is true. I treated her and I'm the one who diagnosed her. I tell you, she was lucky to have me as her doctor. I ordered her a PET scan, because she didn't suspect a thing," Dr. Ramsey confided in them.

"So what's wrong with her? She had surgery so she must be doing better," Betsy hoped.

"You would think so, but I don't hope any more, not in her condition. You should know she has Stage IV lung cancer. She is in ICU, probably dying by now." Dr. Ramsey's whisper was sad and he almost cried looking at the shocked faces surrounding him.

Betsy decided to call University Hospital's information but she was told "The patient no longer was in the hospital". Betsy started to cry. She barely could answer between sobbing that Dr. Redcliff was not there, she probably died by then.

The rumor spread like wildfire and everyone felt bad about losing her. The employees had an ongoing collection for sending flowers for her expected funeral. In the interim the ICU nurses elevated Dr. Ramsey to a new moral and medical pedestal to do so much for her before the unexpected end. Dr. Ramsey very modestly brushed them off with an "Ah, you shouldn't, that's what I do for all my patients, and especially for my colleague. She and I were best friends," was his response.

Marsha had no idea that she had the nicest eulogies said behind her back. Dr. Verdi removed her chest tubes and some of her sutures without as much as a twinge of pain. While he sat on her bed and pleasantly chatted with her, she didn't notice that his skilled hands had worked so fast on turning her lose. He was just as excellent in dexterity as in deterring his patient's attention.

When she got up and felt a bit dizzy, a very opinionated cleaning lady called for a nurse by announcing, "The patient got lightheaded, probably was nothing serious, only her *electric lights* were off. You need to check them."

The nurse angrily brushed her off by snapping, "You should mind your own business and finish cleaning the room," and turned to Marsha with an indignant, "Can you imagine? She is telling me what to do? Electric lights! Yeah, that's what I should check. Last week she called a Petri-dish a peach-tree-dish. What's next?"

As it turned out, the cleaning lady was correct; Marsha's electrolytes needed a boost. She quietly wrapped up the lesson she learned: one never should ignore any input, no matter how ridiculous or incorrect it might sound. The cleaning lady may not have used the correct terms but she heard enough medicine during her work to know what could cause a problem. She had an innate intelligence which was more than what some people had in the educated echelon of health care, concluded Marsha.

Evidently she was improving because her spunkiness slowly returned. It must have been a little Devil whispering to her to tell Dr. Verdi, "You know I always wondered how you performed extensive surgery while only making such small incision. It truly amazes me. Look at your hands, they're pretty big!" She said it as a joke, but apparently the humor flew over Dr. Verdi's head.

Although he seemed to be startled by the presumed ignorance of another physician, he replied with total sincerity, "I did not put my hand in the wound. We have instruments for that."

Marsha busted out in laughter, holding onto her side. If it hurt her it was worth every second of pain.

Dr. Verdi realized the jest and eased his solemn expression into a grin, "You'll be OK now, I am convinced. You are a tough, old bird."

"Gosh, it sounds like I need to be carbon dated next." Marsha tried to joke over her shock. She never would have expected Dr. Verdi say that to her, though he might have meant it in a warm, friendly manner, and without the slightest intention to offend.

"Before I let you go home, let's talk seriously. You know I had to remove the lower lobe of your right lung. This had the cancer. On the good news, none of the lymph nodes were positive and there was no metastasis anywhere. You had a Stage I/B adenocarcinoma of the lung. Pretty good staging, wouldn't you say so?"

"Great!" Said Marsha, instantly realizing how awkward her response to a fatal disease sounded.

"On the other hand, you had a problem in the upper lobe," continued Dr. Verdi.

"Metastasis?" Probed Marsha.

"No, no cancer there."

"Thank God!" She began to breathe easier.

"I am not through, yet," Dr. Verdi calmly carried on, "You had a pretty extensive, but localized infection in the right upper lobe."

"That's not so bad, is it?" She asked with confidence.

"Unfortunately, I had to remove half of the upper lung so the pathologist could diagnose the cause of that lesion. I just got the phone call, it was MAC. Mycobacterium avium intracellulare." Dr. Verdi and Marsha said the last three words together.

"Probably this was the cause of your chronic cough.

Too bad, they did not diagnose it sooner. If they did, you could have taken medications and still would have the upper lobe intact. On the other hand you were lucky, because that cough led to the cancer discovery. You probably wouldn't have known it otherwise. Not until it was too late. But for the MAC you could have been treated with antibiotics instead losing a quarter of your lung with surgery. I have to admit, you are one unlucky gal to get two critical diseases in the same organ. Furthermore, both present with the same symptoms. How do you like that? As the saying goes, only doctors and nurses get such complex diseases, common people would have one or the other."

"So I was not crazy for complaining about the cough. And it was not a psychogenic cough which was patterned into my mind, either," Marsha felt vindicated.

"Heavens no, it wasn't. That would be a pretty unwise idea, wouldn't it?" Dr. Verdi seemed to be baffled by Marsha's remark. Although he didn't ask any questions, he clearly expected some explanations.

"I thought so, too. Imagine, this came from a pretty well-known neurology professor. Actually, it was the Chairman of my residency. Well, never mind, it's in the past. It just hurt when he said it. Dr. Verdi you have no idea how many years I suffered from this cough. Not only by the coughing, itself, but also by the humiliation and embarrassment it caused. And because it was considered a psychogenic cough, some of my professors went out of their way to shame me. I tried so hard to get help. Would you believe, Dr. Ramsey was my eighth pulmonologist? Never in my life would I ever return to him. He, just like the rest, only copied each other's misdiagnosis and paid no attention to me. He said my coughing was due to bronchiectasis and it didn't get better because I was non-compliant with the inhalers and cough syrups. I am glad to know what was going on finally. Now we have the correct diagnosis. So what's next? What do I have to do now? Take some antibiotics?"

The last question shook Dr. Verdi from his quiet reflection of what Marsha revealed. He felt thankful to discuss the future treatments instead of being possibly confronted on incompetent colleagues and foolish ideas presented as diagnosis.

"No, it won't be necessary. Don't forget, the whole area was resected and I made sure it was cut out with a wide margin. Of course, you have to recover from the surgery first. I will see you in my office in two weeks. In the interim make an appointment with a pulmonologist to follow-up with you. You could go to Dr. Stale. His office is in the hospital."

Marsha gingerly sat in the wheelchair, wincing at every bump on the way to the parking lot. After two weeks in ICU it was good to see the sunshine, feel the breeze, and be part of the living once more. As she was transferring to the car an ambulance pulled up and unloaded a stretcher. The stretcher was covered by a sheet; apparently the person did not make it. A tall, older man climbed out of the ambulance and for a second looked at Marsha, then sadly followed the stretcher to the building. Marsha felt a chill running down on her spine and was the more thankful to regain her own life.

She was grateful to be discharged from the hospital and looked forward to start the long recuperation at home.

25

Amicus certus in re incerta cernitur.
A true friend proves to be certain in the uncertain times.
_____
Roman proverb

Debbie arrived and with her infectious laughter and cheerful chatting, the quiet day of cautious recovery suddenly disappeared. It was impossible to remain sad, solemn, or depressed in her presence. She sat near Marsha, who rested on the reclining sofa. Sonna was busy preparing a fruit tray and ice tea.

"I am so glad you could come from California, Sonna," stated Debbie, "Marsha would not be able to recover at home if you were not here. Imagine," she turned to Marsha, "you would be in some rehab center fighting for the right order of food or getting your medication on time. I had plenty of experiences with my mom and saw what they do there. I guess it's great for people who can't be taken care of at home, like the very ill who still need nursing care or those who are alone. You are a great friend for doing it, Sonna."

"Of course, what are friends for? I knew I was needed as soon as I heard you decided to recover at home after your surgery." She looked at Marsha, "How could you think you could? You are not too bright, my friend, thinking you could manage it alone." She shook her head at Marsha disapprovingly.

"OK, I know, I know the 'Spirit is willing but the flesh is weak.' But I really thought that between the visits of my friends, somehow I could have made it." In retrospect getting spoiled by Sonna's care, Marsha realized she was not planning her recovery reasonably, by any means.

"Hey, this visiting reminds me, who did you see at your bedside after the surgery?" Debbie asked Marsha.

"You mean before Sonna's arrival? I can only recall Andy, Diana, and you. Why?"

"You suddenly reached out to the right as if holding onto someone or wanting to touch someone, then you opened your eyes as big as a saucer and finally you relaxed again and fell asleep. You repeated the same thing a few times during the first three days. I got curious about what was going on and asked you, 'Do you see anyone by your bedside?' And you replied, 'Yes, can't you see him right beside me?' But there was no one else in the room.

"I thought maybe your mother's spirit came to protect you, but you shook your head 'no'. I kept telling you it was your mother who had come back to stay with you and watch over you and maybe the person who visited you was a 'she' and not a 'he' as you said. Maybe you made a mistake. But you shook your head and vehemently insisted on this was someone else. You never revealed who you saw, though. Who was he?"

Marsha always ended with a fuzzy, warm, inner feeling after she had a fading dream of her late mother. Although the image soon disappeared in the morning, the cozy feeling remained with her for the whole day. She was certain the hospital vision could not have belonged to her mom because even if she could not recall her, she thought she would have retained some comforting sensation.

Finally, Debbie decided, "Maybe you were right. Maybe it was not anyone you knew from before." She contemplated on Marsha's answers for a few minutes, turning them over in her mind a couple of times before she blurted out, "Oh, I've got it! If it was not your mother then it was your guardian angel. When you came out of surgery and after the many complications you had in the first few days, you had to have a protective force next to you, defending you from all possible harm. This must have been who you saw standing there right by your side, protecting you where you had been cut open."

"What are you talking about?" Marsha did not consider or particularly believe that there was a guardian spirit next to her though to survive the major surgery with such favorable outcome surely was miraculous. "What made you think I was familiar with him?"

Debbie replied with confidence, "Because you looked to the right without any surprise or fear. And you were sort of comfortable with what you saw. I am sure you knew who was standing there. You even attempted to talk to him. I saw your lips moving and you smiled as you listened to him. Then, eventually you relaxed and fell back on the pillow. That's why originally I thought perhaps it was your mom."

"Maybe I just reached out to stretch my arms..." Marsha was searching for a logical explanation.

"No, it could not have been an accident. It was done on purpose. You tried to grasp at something or grab someone on your right. It had to have a special meaning or importance for you because you even used the side that hurt you the most." Debbie was more than convinced that what she had witnessed was a perplexing, invisible, miraculous vision only Marsha could see.

Maybe Debbie was right, Marsha concluded. She no longer doubted her but unfortunately, she could not recall the events at all. When she tried to look back, her mind appeared to be a freshly erased board; a genuine *tabula rasa*.

Debbie continued, "After that you had a sound sleep, the first real long and restful sleep you got. If it was not your mother, then I am convinced it was your guardian angel."

Marsha started to accept Debbie's reasoning. Half of what her friend said seemed logical or at least was thought-provoking. The other half required blind faith.

"OK, if it was my protecting angel, why couldn't he stay? I was still quite ill, not nearly back to half of my normal self. Couldn't this Gabriel or Raphael hang around a bit longer?" Marsha was still skeptical.

"He did his duty. Once you had improved enough, he could continue to safeguard you invisibly from a distance. Don't worry, he still watches over you. You just can't see him anymore. Don't forget, you are no longer in a halfway place – one leg with us and the other on the other side. You know, being in sort of a limbo. Now that time is over and you have returned fully to the living." Debbie was very persuasive and she evidently believed every word she said. "We can't discern angels when we use our eyes and not our spirits. I believe in them. Don't you?"

Sonna whole-heartedly agreed with Debbie. She also believed in guardian angels who were ordered to protect us, to spread their huge wings in defense as they hovered above and fended off the evil spirits.

Marsha took a good long look at her friends. Debbie's eyes were blue, her hair blonde, and she radiated loyalty, faithfulness, and reliance. She stood by her since the first day of her ordeal began. Sonna left her husband and put her life on hold to take care of her after her discharge from the hospital. The moment she heard Marsha's predicament, she immediately volunteered to help. Prior to her discharge, she guarded her friend with the fierce protective instinct of a tigress: she made sure Marsha's privacy was maintained and her dietary orders were carried out correctly. Both Debbie and Sonna had the unshakable confidence of belief written on their face. *Maybe angels came in different shapes and forms*, Marsha thought.

Mulling over Debbie's disclosure, Marsha admitted it was possible she had an out-of-world visitor. She could not come up with a more plausible, scientific explanation. Anyone else on hearing about her actions would have cited hallucinations, drug-induced vision, or the after-effect of anesthesia, but neither Debbie nor Sonna believed in any of them. What the logical, scientific mind rejected, the spirit had to bow to: maybe she was truly protected by a guardian angel.

Since she found no better explanation for the events, Marsha accepted Debbie's theory. Perhaps it was really Raphael or Gabriel who stood by her bedside. Could it be true? Why not? If she felt sheltered while healthy and foolish, would she not deserve even more the impenetrable shield when she was older and ill? At the end, among all the insecurities, doubts and unanswered questions, she only knew with certainty one thing: her heavenly messenger surely earned early retirement for performing way beyond the call of duty on her behalf.

She concluded both young and old were beloved children of the Creator and as much as He loved one, He loved the other, too.

26

*Experience is what you get when
you don't get what you want.*
———
Dan Stanford

Dr. Verdi was tired but his office schedule was full for the afternoon. Looking at the list of patients yet to be seen, he realized it would be a late night again before he would get home. Simultaneously, he almost heard his wife's endless complaints of never getting home before dark, the dinner needed to be reheated, all the household problems fell only on her shoulders, and she was not getting any help from him. Almost subconsciously, he slowed down by talking to each patient about not only their surgical problems but everything else. As if he did not want to go home, he thought. Then it occurred to him that maybe he truly did not want to face his wife.

How much easier life would be if she could just find something to occupy her time; something to keep her busy whether it was a job or volunteer work? Even a garden society would do it. Just to have a life other than focusing on him. Not that her attention was not welcome. After all, catering to her hard-working husband was just and right. Didn't he work from dawn to dusk for her well-being? Didn't he restore health and gave back life to his patients?

The new operating room technician was dead-on when she said,"Oh my, you are just like a god, you create life! You ooze goodness. How lucky are those who come to you!" She was a new addition to the OR staff, but if this gal could appreciate him wouldn't it be fair to say he should get some recognition in his own home, too? He recalled the technician's gentle touch as she tapped the beads of perspiration off of his forehead during surgery... She really paid attention to him. She seemed to understand him.

For a second, he recalled her faint and delicate perfume and soft fingers then shook his head. Thinking of another woman, no matter how attractive or kind she might be, was not in the best interest of a married man. Even if this married man's life was tied into an unhappy marriage.

Yet, his thoughts regularly returned to her, recalling every minuscule interaction. No matter, how much he scolded himself for thinking of her and repeatedly told himself that he should remember he was married. He realized he actually looked forward his days in the operating room which was a different anticipation than before. How would this feeling end and where would it lead him? He recalled she recently noticed he was quiet and looked sad. He should have accepted her offer to talk to her. He decided to say yes to her if she ever approached him again. She would understand and value him. If only his wife could be half as thoughtful... He sighed and entered the next examination room.

Marsha Redcliff was waiting for him and a petite, pretty woman sat close to her. Dr. Verdi pleasantly greeted her, then introduced himself to her friend Sonna, and opened the discussion with "So have you been friends for long?

You two must be close for you to come all the way from California to her rescue."

"Oh, we met ten years ago, on an airplane. Do you want to hear about it?" Marsha asked.

"Sure, it sounds interesting." Dr. Verdi expectantly leaned back on his chair.

"I was going for my mother's funeral and Sonna with her husband was taking a trip to Europe. Don't ask me where they were heading because these two globe-trotters are always going somewhere." She turned to look at Sonna, "Is there any place you two haven't been so far, Sonna? Probably not." Marsha smiled at her friend.

"Oh yes, there is. We haven't been to Antarctica yet, but Fred is scheduling a trip next year to go there. Right after we checked off Machu Picchu from our bucket-list." Sonna turned to Dr. Verdi and explained almost apologetically, "My husband just loves to travel and in about every four to five months he is ready to take another trip or he probably would not survive."

"So as a courtesy of the airline, we sat beside each other," Marsha continued, "Fred tried a few times to strike up a conversation with me but I was afraid I might burst into tears if I talked, so I sort of dismissed his attempts. Then the stewardess brought our dinners and asked who wanted coffee. I held up my cup and as she poured the steaming liquid, the plane tilted and I dumped the whole cup of hot coffee on Fred's lap. You should have seen the mess! The dinner trays flew in every direction as Fred jumped up to brush the coffee off of his pants. We all tried to dab it off of him. I was mortified."

"Really, she apologized so profusely that even Fred felt bad for her," laughed Sonna.

"That's when I told them why I was traveling. The rest of the way Fred kept talking to me to keep my mind off of the funeral. When I returned home, he called to ask how everything went and if I needed any help. Ever since we have been friends." Marsha concluded the story.

"We actually came to visit her in Cecilia Beach and the next year she came to stay with us in California" said Sonna. "When I heard her predicament my first thought was only natural that I should come immediately. Really, she needed someone and I was able to help."

"That's fantastic. It sounds like a fairy-tale friendship. It's nice to know there are good people around like you," he complimented Sonna. "Thank you for helping Marsha."

Then he turned to Marsha, "So how are you doing young lady?"

Hmm, he called her a "young lady" when Sonna was around, while her hair was done and she was dressed to the nines, but he named her a "tough old bird" when he last saw her in the hospital gown without make up...Men. This is so typical of a man. The thoughts flashed through Marsha's mind.

"Have you seen Dr. Stale yet?" Dr. Verdi scribbled something in her chart.

"Yes."

"And?" He looked up from his writing. "Did you like him?"

"He has the personality of a piano leg." Marsha blurted out. As soon as she heard her own words she regretted saying them, but by then it was too late. Dr. Verdi barely was able to suppress his amusement. Marsha quickly added, "I didn't care one way or another, after all I don't go home with him and I don't have to look at his sourpuss face. But truly, I expected him to be a bit nicer. Of course, none of this matters as long as he is as good as you said."

"I believe he is. I told him about your case, we all should be on the same page from here on," Dr. Verdi assured her.

Marsha kept quiet about her less than satisfactory experience with Dr. Stale. Maybe she should give him another chance, she decided. Especially since Dr. Verdi talked to him, he would be more considerate to her.

On her next visit Dr. Stale listened to her lungs on four spots and concluded there was nothing else to do. She was on her way to a complete and total recovery. When Marsha complained of the return of her frequent coughing spells and a lately developed aching pain just below her shoulder blade, he easily replied, "Oh, this is common, it's only from the healing tissues." To her objections he gave her a rather persuasive explanation of post-surgical pain which would cause these symptoms and asked if she wanted pain medications.

Marsha hated pain medications and unless she really needed them she refused to take any. Even in her practice she seldom used them and if the heavy-duty pain killers were indicated she referred her patients to pain management. Of course, it was always simpler for the busy doctors to scribble a prescription of possibly addictive drugs then take time to teach a patient of alternate methods of symptom management. The result could be devastating but that was way down the line in the distant future and was not put into the equation. In her experience, quick concluding doctors created the post-operative drug addicts by indiscriminately prescribing opioids. She did not want to become a doctor's victim again.

"No thanks, I don't want to mask the pain, I would rather like to know the cause of it," she replied as she recalled given multiple inhalers and cough syrups for her cancer and infection caused cough.

"I told you, it's from the surgery. Take the prescription and you'll be perfectly fine."

"Can I have a CT scan instead?" Marsha was obstinate by not agreeing with Dr. Stale. He grudgingly agreed.

Two weeks later he called with the CT findings. Marsha had a renewed MAC infection. The current lesion was in the remaining portion of her upper lung, abutting the lining of her chest, exactly where she felt the pain. Dr. Stale assured Marsha that he reviewed the films with Dr. Verdi who said the findings had nothing to do with cancer, instead it was caused by the recurrent infection.

"Aha, so dear smart-ass Stale was not sure of himself, he had to ask for verification," Marsha shared her conclusion with Sonna.

Marsha already disliked him when he pompously argued with her about Dr. Verdi only removed her lower lobe. According to Dr. Stale, "Nothing was done to your upper lobe. Where did you get this preposterous idea?"

Marsha calmly told him to read the operative report. In return, he angrily looked up the record right in front of him, but instead of his intended proof, he discovered himself to be wrong. To bring his embarrassing lack of knowledge to the open certainly did not put Marsha on his most favorite patient's list.

After that incident, Dr. Stale tried to schedule her next visit with his nurse practitioner, but Marsha categorically refused to see a mid-level person ever again, stating, "Dr. Verdi recommended you and not your nurse practitioner. If you are not able to see me in the future, then I will find a physician who would."

Dr. Stale steadily piled up the bad impressions he made by his non-caring behavior and quick, often incorrect, simple solutions he offered. If Marsha did not insist on the diagnostic test and only took his pain medications, the infection would have rotted out the remaining right lung and spread to both sides. Instead, now she had to be treated by three different antibiotics for two years. Not trusting Dr. Stale any more, she made an appointment to get a second opinion by the University Infectious Diseases Department. It was only after the specialist confirmed the need of the drugs and corrected Dr. Stale's prescribed insufficient dose, that she became satisfied with her treatment.

She decided Dr. Stale was not the kind of physician she would recommend to anyone and especially not for herself. He only confirmed that in a medical school's ranking the last to graduate was also called "doctor" and at the end he proved that anyone could be a doctor. She never returned to his office again.

27

What lies behind us and what lies before us
are small matters compared to what lies within us.

Ralph Waldo Emerson

With Sonna's help, Marsha returned to Cecilia Beach Hospital and first stopped by to visit the ICU. All the nurses and EEG technicians gathered around her and then as the news of her presence traveled through the hospital, more employees came by to see her. It was a warm welcome back, a real homecoming celebration.

"My you look great! Slimmed down a bit and looking good. Now you could be a fashion model," greeted her Josè.

"Well the weight loss by itself doesn't quite qualify me for that," Marsha smiled.

"When I grow up I want to be like you!" One of the salt-and-pepper haired nurses interjected.

"Thanks, but you are just fine as you are," said Marsha. Then she turned to Josè and added, "To be a fashion model, I would have to grow at least five more inches or grow at least three more vertebrae. It's highly unlikely that any of these would happen in the near future."

"No, you may only need two inches because the high

heels would make up for the rest! Gosh, how can you walk on those heels?"

"Josè you are a man and wouldn't understand it. Just give up and enjoy the sight."

Marsha felt safe to use the lighthearted tone with Josè who openly declared Dr. Redcliff as his favorite physician. Besides, he was younger than Marsha's children so she usually took on a motherly jesting with him.

Betsy rushed to hug her then quickly stepped back and apologized in case she hurt her. "I'm so glad you are here! Tell us how you feel. Be quiet all of you."

After Marsha assured them she was feeling great, her recovery was on schedule and her spirit remained intact, Betsy hesitatingly questioned her," So you are not dying, are you?"

"No, I am not going to give my enemies the satisfaction if I can help it," replied Marsha then continued seriously, "What gave you this idea? You see that I am alive and kicking, I will stick around for a while. I am not good enough to be an angel to be accepted in Heaven and I certainly hope I am not bad enough for Hell, so I'll just have to stay here."

"We were told you had Stage IV lung cancer and dying in the University Hospital's ICU. I called to inquire but they told me you were not there," Betsy explained.

"I was not there because I was discharged to recover at home. Who told you this foolishness?"

"Your own pulmonologist, Dr. Ramsey. He said unless he diagnosed you, you probably would have keeled over one day not knowing what hit you. You were lucky to be friends."

"Really, he is incredible. Number one: I had Stage I cancer and had no metastasis. Number two: he did not make the diagnosis. As a matter of fact, he missed my diagnosis, altogether. Number three: I knew what my diagnosis was sooner than he did. About the friendship: let me say we were always on a friendly working relationship but never more than that. Hasn't he heard about HIPAA and patient privacy before? I sure don't appreciate him spreading my health history and state of health all over town!" Marsha was fuming.

Betsy quickly switched the topic to the ICU patients. Poor Mr. Donlevy died of complications of his Lou Gehrig disease shortly after Marsha took ill. His wife donated all his belongings, and brought a huge bouquet of flower to the nurses. She asked about Dr. Redcliff, but when she was told the doctor was having a surgery, she wished her a speedy recovery and was gone.

One of Marsha's old patients, Valerie Booth, was admitted four days prior with an intracranial hemorrhage and never recovered from her emergent brain surgery. Her blood pressure and heart rate slowly trended toward the level of being incompatible with life and now it was just a matter of hours when she stopped living. Marsha asked them if she could see the eighty-five-year-old lady.

Marsha was surprised to see her resting completely still in bed. Valerie looked like a pale, marble statue and if she didn't know better, she would have thought the old lady was asleep. Then she noted the hallmark of being in ICU: each body orifice had some sort of tube attached to and both of her arms infused vitamin and electrolyte enriched fluid. Her head was wrapped in a heavy white gauze dressing which covered her like a huge turban. Near-death was kind to her because all her wrinkles disappeared and she looked decades younger. Marsha glanced at the bedside monitor and realized the end was fast approaching: her heart rate registered thirty-four beats and her blood pressure was in an unacceptably low range of fifty-two over forty.

Marsha stood by her bedside watching the peaceful

body of her patient and friend who slowly parted from everything known to her. If death could ever be called nice, then hers was a nice death: calm, peaceful, dignified, and noble. As she recalled many of their discussions suddenly she remembered she made a promise to sing at her funeral a song from a Latin mass. During one of her visits, maybe two years prior, Valerie Booth talked to her about the day when she was ill as a little girl. Her father sang *Pange Lingua Gloriosi* to her until she fell asleep. When she woke up she felt better and the illness crisis was over. Valerie always wanted this song to be sung at her funeral believing she would have a peaceful rest then but none of her friends knew either the Latin words or the music.

Surprised at her own boldness Marsha volunteered to do it. She happened to know the song. Valerie happily agreed although she readily dismissed her doctor's placating words that many more years would pass before she would have to sing it.

Now Dr. Redcliff softly started to hum the song. *Why wait for the funeral? Valerie would not hear it then but maybe she could detect some of it now. Even if she could not process the words or recall the meaning of the words, the sounds might give her a little comfort while parting,* thought Marsha.

She just began the second verse when she felt Betsy tugging at her dress. She turned back to the nurse but she stared at the monitor while pointing at the flashing numbers. Valerie Booth's blood pressure rose to eighty-two over fifty, her heart rate was fifty-four. On her unchanged face a small tear drop rolled down from under the tightly closed eye lids. When Marsha finished the song, her vital signs slowly dropped to the prior low level. Three hours later she quietly passed away.

When Betsy and Dr. Redcliff returned to the nurses'

station, all gathered around them again. The nurses interrupted each other as they all wanted to tell her about their work, grumbled of the number of patients assigned to them, and cautiously criticized the ICU doctors. "They don't spend the same time with the patients, not like you do. They just rush through the orders and disappear. They leave to us to talk with the families. It's just not right to dump that responsibility on us."

"Of course they rush off, Dr. Ramsey covers two hospitals beside us and has a Pulmonary Function Clinic, plus his office patients."

"Dr. Ramsey is also busy in administration, he is the Chairman of the whole medical department here, don't forget that. You cannot expect him to have time for the patients, too," Betsy said with searing sarcasm.

Next they revealed that the many information channels between the University Hospital and Cecilia Beach Hospital worked overtime with the news of Dr. Verdi's separation. Actually, some nurses heard that by now he moved out of his home, presumably because of an OR technician. His house was listed for sale. One of the hospitalists already toured it with a real estate agent, but found it too high priced, way out of his budget. Marsha was stunned hearing the gossip. From the moment she met Dr. Verdi, she placed him on a soaring tall pedestal. She also gave him such an eminent position which probably was humanly impossible to maintain for long. As she discovered that his private life and his professional achievements did not go hand in hand, first she was dubious, then disappointed in Dr. Verdi. At the end, she only felt genuinely sad about the turmoil of his life caused by a pending divorce.

She calmly remarked. "One would never know what can happen in life, just as one never would know what made him come to the decision he made. I only hope he will find what he's looking for."

Marsha listened with interest to the in-house stories and all the concerns of the nurses. They bitterly accounted Mr. Lawler's announcement of no raise to be given this year to the employees. He blamed the economy, the many regulations the hospital was forced to implement and as a result, did not meet the projected profit. He tried to sweeten the unexpected blow by promising a general raise in the following year. He praised the "family of employees" and encouraged them to continue their excellent work. As the CEO of the facility, he promised to work with them toward this rewarding, great, future goal. Marsha had to bite her tongue knowing the effect of tight economy somehow eluded the CEO because he took home his six million dollar bonus, as usual.

She recalled hearing that the administrator's bonus depended on the number of health insurance contracts the hospital recommended. When the Cecilia Beach Hospital network funded their own health insurance, naturally, the work place switched the employee benefits to their own insurance. In addition, each patient was approached to change his policy and get coverage from the novel insurance which gave an extraordinary good deal to the buyer and the seller alike. The main selling gimmick was a simple question added to a very convincing sales pitch: "Wouldn't you rather stay within the family of the Cecilia Beach system? When you need to be hospitalized, you wouldn't have to worry, because your own doctors would treat you in the hospital. It would practically be the same as if you were in your doctor's office: a continuation of care so nothing would be missed." With the mushrooming satellite clinics and nearby sister-hospitals the Cecilia Beach Health Care system eventually developed monopoly of the entire county's health care and insurance.

Marsha was not sure if this project did not merit collusion. Yet, she never heard anyone mentioning, or God forbid, challenging it. Maybe this was one of the good reasons why the hospital kept three, full time lawyers on staff. She had to admit, it was a shrewd move; after all, money was transferred from one pocket to the next of the same coat. And whether the transaction occurred left to right or right to left, the coat's owner benefitted a certain percentage from each transfer. It was capitalism at its best while all along only democratic slogans were voiced to the public. The gravy tray kept being refilled almost as if by miracle to those near the table.

Marsha also learned to her greatest surprise that Sarah was let go. Mr. Lawler apparently had enough of her meddling and after he accidentally found Sarah's secret book on the desk, he asked for her resignation. The hospital grapevine knew about the CEO very diplomatically never mentioning her secretary's clandestine record-keeping but instead, he used the loss of Dr. Pacheco to his advantage and to the demise of Sarah.

He sternly reminded the secretary of the many occasions when Dr. Pacheco bitterly complained of Sarah harassing her at work and generally made her hospital days and work miserable. At the end, he stated, the relentless bullying left the neurologist no other alternative but to resign. By that time Mr. Lawler kept referring to Dr. Pacheco as an irreplaceable asset to the company whose loss was Sarah's fault alone. He conveniently omitted the fact that neither he nor Dr. Marlene ever made any changes to ease the neurologist's work. The promises and the nice words, along with their originating sources, totally lost the initial credibility.

At the end of the CEO's speech, Dr. Pacheco was

almost elevated to sainthood, while Sarah had left no redeeming features. It was inevitable that Mr. Lawler had to act with draconic measures if the health care family was to continue as a family. Although he was saddened by the step he was forced to take, as the CEO of the organization, he was obligated to protect the other physicians from similar fate. Sarah was quickly replaced with a new secretary who remained invisible to the hospital staff.

To change the sensitive subject Marsha inquired of the others missing from this welcoming group. She learned Cathy went on maternity leave and Ivy and Kelly quit. She warmly congratulated Josè who recently received the Daisy Award in recognition of his excellence in nursing.

"I am so proud of you my friend. If anyone ever deserved this recognition, it is you," Marsha complimented him. Josè's skin darkened with the blood rushing to his face and he awkwardly shook Marsha's hand as he accepted the public praise.

"If you ever decide to go back to school and become a nurse practitioner, let me know. I want to be the first to recommend you." Josè replied, he was not sure but lately he was thinking of the idea.

They told her under the greatest secrecy that about two months after she left, Chuck Potts was arrested. He injected the IV of an old, quite ill man with potassium chloride and the man died of a cardiac arrest. Chuck was not caught red-handed in the act although an unexplained vial of potassium and a used syringe was found in his pocket. Unbeknownst to him, by that time they continuously watched him because it seemed the really ill patients always died on his shift. No one knew when his court case was to be scheduled or whether it was open for the public to attend or not. Since then the hospital changed the drug formulary: potassium was no longer available on the nursing units and only the pharmacy could dispense the premixed IV fluids.

They all were in agreement that Dave Cooper had a justified law suit against Dr. Ferguson and Cecilia Beach Hospital because he ended up pretty bad after his stroke. He lost half of his vision, was unable to use his dominant hand, and could not walk without assistance. Truly, the initial recommendation should have been followed by the ER doctor. Mr. Cooper's attorney was like a blood hound on the track of a bleeding animal because he went where the money was and sued for multi millions of dollars. He claimed as a result of the missed clot-busting medication, his client lost his ability to work and became an invalid. Everyone knew what the outcome of the legal suit had to be. Marsha was thankful she was not named in the suit.

Dr. Gupta, the arrogant orthopedic surgeon was escorted out of the operating suite in hand cuffs. Apparently, the two years investigating Medicare fraud yielded more than enough evidence for his arrest. The nurses all knew his own physician's assistant was the whistle-blower.

"The case was immediately published by the State Department of Health and Medical Board. I guess that should scare off the other wannabe medical criminals." Betsy was visibly indignant.

"Oh my God! This was the same Dr. Gupta whom I was advised to follow! Mr. Lawler told me Dr. Gupta should be my example and that I should stick to his methods to increase my productivity. Would you believe he recorded eighty patients per day when he worked in the clinic? No wonder he was Mr. Lawler's idol. Imagine the money he raked in every day!" Marsha still felt offended.

"Eighty? That's ten patients per hour. He had to see a

new patient in every six minutes, examine and interview them, review their X-rays and CT scan images, and complete all his dictation. Impossible," claimed Josè.

"Wait a second," yelled the EEG technician, "This means for eight hours he did not stop to eat or make a phone call or use the men's room."

"Maybe he had a catheter," Josè shrugged his shoulder. Then he turned to Dr. Redcliff, "See what happens when you are away? You have to come back and you have to do it soon. We all miss you."

On the way home Sonna adamantly urged her to seek legal help because she concluded it was simply criminal to what Dr. Ramsey subjected her to. She reminded Marsha that both Dr. Verdi and Dr. Murphy expressed their disbelief so it was not only her friend who saw the injustice. The latest intrusion of her privacy was only the proverbial cherry on the cake. It was the final insult that ultimately pushed Marsha to consult a malpractice attorney.

28

The law is a horrible business.

Clarence Darrow

The third law firm finally was willing to listen to Marsha's complaint. The first two just dragged their feet for weeks with "researching the background" but at the end declined to help. All admitted that Marsha was wronged and had a firm legal case but neither wanted to risk their money for her. The second attorney happened to be a woman and probably sympathized with her a bit, before she finally explained to Marsha the practical side of the law.

Esq. Abigail McIntosh was brutally honest when she explained the required financial investments a lawyer has to make before getting any reimbursement.

"Let's pretend we take your case on a contingency or 30 percent of the awarded sum. We would have to get expert witnesses, arrange and participate in all depositions, file the claim at various authorities, and I'm not even speaking hereof the fee for the innumerable hours it takes to prepare the case. These all cost an exorbitant sum of money." She tapped the desk with her pen at each item just to emphasize it.

"Look, a single deposition may last for eight hours and in your case I estimate at least four will be needed with the added cost of a Court reporter and videotaping. Do you have any idea how much an expert witness charges? Usually $600-800 per hour just to review the material and a $1000 and above for the deposition itself." Her tapping became crisper and louder as she continued her explanation.

"A small firm like ours could not afford such risky investments. Furthermore, you have to realize the projected reimbursement was iffy because not one person could ever bank on a Court's verdict or the opinion of jurors. So to take a chance meant enormous hazard and unless there were mitigating factors we would politely have to decline the case."

"What mitigating factors are you referring? Help me out here; I don't know what you mean." Marsha pleaded with the attorney.

"Look, I agree with you, you were wronged. Let me explain to you in simple terms so you understand me." Marsha winced at the condescending tone, but realizing she was the "beggar" and the attorney was the "begee," she kept quiet.

The self-assured lawyer smoothly slid onto a higher academic level and continued, "Every malpractice suit has two components: first we have to establish negligence and second we have to see the financial consequences. There is no question in my mind you would win the negligence part of the suit. But you practically had no financial losses, so what could we claim as damage, your suffering? You recovered and you are fine. You are back to work. Actually, you went back too soon, in three months. That was a big mistake. You did not get either a prolonged nursing care or a psychological counseling, not even a service dog, or some sort of assistance. Another blunder. Huge! In other words everything is the same as before. Am I correct?"

"Heavens, no," Marsha replied in a huff, "I lost my private patients to another neurologist, I had to close my office and I lost three-quarter of my income. I could never continue my practice, but would have to begin to build it up again. I would have to start from square one as if I were a fresh graduate or new in the area. So I lost a lot!"

"It's hard to prove what could have been, should have been, or would have been. Let me spell it out for you: you had not lost enough financially to make the case lucrative enough for us to take. Sorry, this is my final decision." She put down the pen indicating she finished the interview.

Marsha stood up and looked straight into the attorney's eyes, "So where are all the TV lawyers and all the media cases of malpractice suits? Where are the Perry Masons, the Frank Galvins, or the persistent detectives of Monk or Lieutenant Columbo? I realize, these are TV entertainments, but many episodes were based on true facts. I have also worked in Workman's compensation cases, so I know what benefits a simple muscle strain ends up with and it's nowhere as serious as my injury was."

"C'mon, you don't believe in the few famous litigations spread all over the newspapers, do you? Those people probably stayed out of work and got every possible assistance to pad their claim by the time the attorney got involved. Your problem was you were too honest."

"Am I being penalized for not milking the system? Essentially what you're saying is, the moral victory is mine. That's all? I just realized my life was less important than your pocket. Nice to know. Thanks for your time." Her whole body was shaking and she had to sit in her car for a while to calm down before she attempted to pull out from the parking lot.

After much research and almost when she was ready to toss in the towel, she was referred to the Monty Law Firm. It was two counties away and had no connection to the Cecilia Beach health care providers. Mr. Monty had firsthand experience of a similar family history; his father also died of a misdiagnosed lung cancer. He recommended bringing a law suit against the involved physician but his mother refused it. She liked the doctor and didn't want to bring him any harm, as she said, "It was enough that he had to live with his conscience." Mr. Monty wondered whether the physician had enough conscience to bother him at all.

After listening to Marsha's sad saga, he went gang ho. "Oh, your dear Dr. Ramsey has no idea what is about to hit him! We are going to be so prepared and efficient to drag him through the mud, to punish him, just the way he deserves it. You will see, trust me. You have a solid case, so I wouldn't worry about what that McIntosh lawyer said to you. Our firm has many years of legal experience in such cases and we successfully represented many clients in Court, because we like to win. We can serve your doctor exactly the medication which he rightfully deserves."

By signing a three page contract, Marsha agreed to the Monty Law Firm and particularly to Mr. Wayne O. Monty, Esq., to provide her with legal representation in the case of Marsha Redcliff, MD vs. Nahab Ramsey, MD and Hiroto Katsui, MD. The law firm only would receive a small fraction of the recovered sum, 34 percent to be exact, and Mr. Monty would seek enough money to cover every additional expense as well, for sure.

A week later another attorney arrived to obtain an initial interview with Marsha. He appeared to be more of a clerk than a lawyer, totally bland and insignificant, not at all what Marsha expected. He doggedly unearthed every detail of her illness, surgery, and subsequent recovery. At the end of the long day, thinking of the seven hours she spent with the man, Marsha wondered why the meeting had to take place in her home. The only reason she saw might have been a discreet estimation of her living conditions, learning whether her statements jived with the real life facts and conditions or she padded her story with unsustainable details. Sly lawyers; all of them are sly, she concluded.

The preliminary work slowly dragged along. Finally a year later she was scheduled for deposition. The previous months were filled with innumerable requests to provide proofs of every minute statement and copies of documents from every phase of her life. Marsha had difficulty to find all of her records of education, marriage and divorce decrees, addresses of her previous residences, and daily work schedule. If these were not cumbersome enough then she had to supply the names of all her doctors from the last ten years including their addresses and phone numbers. To complicate the search for the treating physicians even more, while she was hospitalized every contacting physician's name had to be added to the list.

Marsha never met any of the pathologists, laboratory doctors, or ancillary personnel whose names appeared on her medical records, but had to contact each one in order to complete her list. When she complained to Mr. Monty that this and her eye doctors and dentists had nothing to do with her recent pulmonary history, she was told "Dr. Ramsey's attorney has the right to demand that information". In return, she frostily instructed her attorney to demand the same from Dr. Ramsey, but Mr. Monty rejected her request with a simple "It doesn't work that way". Marsha felt she was further victimized and the legal system protected the criminal more than the injured party.

The deposition of Marsha Redcliff, MD went smoothly though it occurred to Marsha there was a spooky similarity between her facing the lawyers of opposition and the lions against Christians in the Roman Colosseum.

"You were terrific," Mr. Monty faced her afterward; "None of their lawyers could get you nervous or upset. You stood your ground for over eight hours. That should be a new record. How did you manage it?"

"Simple: I knew I was right and I said nothing but the truth. How could I be blamed for what happened? Whatever or however long it would take, eventually justice would be served. I am convinced that integrity and honesty couldn't be rewarded with injustice." Marsha replied with unshakeable conviction.

"Well the Goddess of Justice has her eyes covered. Nothing else influences her but what she hears. After today I no longer worry about you. You certainly will make an excellent witness," her lawyer complimented her.

"Thanks, except I am the victim and not the witness," Marsha corrected him.

29

I do not care to speak ill of any man behind his back,
but I believe the gentleman is an attorney.

Samuel Johnson

"So what's next?" Marsha was trained by her highly demanding profession to seek solution after a diagnosis, and search for alternate roads if the one she found herself on was suddenly blocked.

"Next we'll get a deposition from Dr. Ramsey and Dr. Katsui, and then we'll get Dr. Murphy and Dr. Verdi to testify. I predict we'll go to mediation afterward," Mr. Monty projected.

"How about Dr. Ramsey's assistant? She was the one who lied to me first. Don't you want to subpoena her, too?"

"I guess we could but it would be pretty useless because she would say whatever Dr. Ramsey instructed her. Besides, I understood she no longer worked with him. Anyway, I would need her address and phone number to contact her."

"No problem, I can get that. Listen Mr. Monty, I worry about Dr. Ramsey's lawyers. So far they were very aggressive and annoying with their constant unnecessary and unrelated demands. Their belligerence is a good predictor of how they will handle the case." Marsha added.

"Don't worry, we have our ammunition, too. Don't underestimate me."

After a lengthy discussion they agreed that Mr. Monty should obtain Dr. Ramsey's work schedule for the weeks when Marsha was seen in his office. Marsha told him the clinic seemed to be understaffed and was always overbooked. Mr. Monty quickly grabbed the idea to explain this caused the doctor's rush and subsequent oversight. Marsha insisted on the importance of semantics and wanted to use the term "negligence" instead of "oversight". Her attorney agreed.

Almost another year later, when she read Dr. Ramsey's deposition, she was surprised that no question was asked about his busy work days. The more she read the angrier she got. At the end she was fuming, because she realized Dr. Ramsey lied under oath like a child whose hand was caught in the cookie jar. Her legal representor easily brushed away her concerns, by stating "We know he lied. It was obvious."

Marsha was irate, "If you knew he lied, why didn't you point it out? He just got away with it. Isn't it called a perjury? From now on, if ever anyone refers to his deposition and because you didn't make obvious that it was filled with a pack of lies, it would appear as a true statement. After all, it was made under oath, wasn't it? Furthermore, he later could defend himself by saying 'I said it under oath and nothing was objected.' Essentially, you created a 'he-said-she-said' case."

"Well, it was so clear he lied that even the jury would see it. It's not necessary to pick on everything. See the big picture instead or you could get lost in the details," advised Mr. Monty.

"But he stated it was him who recommended me

to get a repeat CT or MR after the first test showed the abnormal findings. How could he say it when he was not even there? Remember, I only saw his nurse practitioner who said everything was the same. Then Ramsey further lied by saying I supposedly replied to him 'Nahab, I had so many tests, I don't want any more radiation.' First of all, he was not present at that visit. Second, never in my life I ever called him by his first name. Third, if it was true what he said then why isn't it in my chart? Didn't you point out that nothing was written in my chart about this new version? Usually if something was not recorded, it was not done. Fourth, was not it I who demanded a PET scan when he only wanted an X-ray? It made no sense that suddenly I supposedly changed and did not care about the radiation affect, did it? He actually put the responsibility and blame on me! Just to prove how he lied, why didn't you at least ask him when did I start calling him by his first name? I have never, ever called him anything, but Dr. Ramsey. Although now I have plenty of choice words I could use to call him!" Marsha raged.

Mr. Monty just smiled, "Calm down or you'll work yourself up to a stroke or a heart attack. I know it and the jury would know it. It's OK; it's so obvious he lied. Trust me; it will all come out at the end."

He ignored Marsha's complaints about the missing work schedule. The nurse practitioner was not even mentioned during the deposition.

Marsha was upset and kept repeating, "Yes, he obviously lied but did you point it out? No. You let him get away with a big, fat, and damaging lie just because it was obvious and you didn't point it out."

"It would have been redundant. We all saw it. When we go to Court the jury and the judge will see it, also. I told you, you are too anxious, calm down. I have extensive court room experience. When we get there you'll be

211

surprised to see me in action. I will ask for nothing less than a couple of million dollars."

The same uneasiness returned to her after Dr. Katsui's deposition. Mr. Monty summarized the deposition, "This young man was very impressive. He talked in clear and concise sentences, very rapidly, and he was unmistakably a very intelligent man. Although he was a bit cocky and had too much self-confidence, but that's OK because that's where a good lawyer can find some firm ground to begin the attack."

However, Marsha heard of no attacks. She realized Mr. Monty was no match for the conceited physician because the attorney clearly lacked the medical knowledge to pursue details or debate the doctor's statements. He even missed Katsui's damning statement about not recommending a PET scan. He did not suggest any following test for the abnormal CT scan because the "PET scan was an expensive test and it cost a lot of money", he stated. Furthermore, he admitted that his company did not perform PET scans. He was adamant never to order any test that he had no way to do. He never considered contacting other facilities which had the capability to carry out the order. Evidently money was more important to him than a patient's life. Marsha, as a non-legal person, picked up the inadvertent confession while Mr. Monty, the lawyer, missed it altogether.

Again, Mr. Monty doused her fear by projecting he finally would use his "big gun" when questioning her two surgeons. Another half a year later his legal secretary notified Marsha of Dr. Verdi's and Dr. Murphy's deposition was scheduled for the following day. She apologized for not giving Marsha longer notice but it was the opposing attorney and not Mr. Monty who requested the deposition. Marsha felt as if she were pushed to the edge of a quick sand pit.

Afterward she learned from Mr. Monty that both Dr. Murphy and Dr. Verdi claimed limited memory of their pre-operative discussion with Marsha. They strictly talked about the actual interventions and customary after care only. They emphasized that their participation was according to the standard medical care and they were neither privileged nor qualified to make comments on anything else.

Mr. Monty appeared to lose hope, "I expected them to support you much more. Especially by admitting that they could have done a less dangerous surgery if you would have been recommended to them sooner. But they limited their answers to their interaction and nothing else. Not good, not good at all."

"Maybe then you should have been in touch with them first and not the insurance attorneys," replied Marsha curtly. "Did you even mention the fact that Dr. Ramsey missed both conditions? Both the cancer and the infection?"

"Well, he treated you with medications, didn't he?"

"And since when was an inhaler a standard care of treatment either for cancer or for a bacterial infection? Did you ever question my doctor why the infection was neglected? As a result of this negligence I lost an additional quarter of my lung instead of being treated by a simple antibiotic. That did not matter?"

A few minutes of silence passed before Mr. Monty finally responded, "Well, we need to concentrate on the cancer, and not every little thing. I told you, you could be lost soon if you try to do everything." A moment later he added, "Don't fret yet, we are not through. The jury might think completely differently. Next we go to Court, or mediation. We'll see whichever comes first."

"What decides it?" Marsha was curious.

"It's all depending on how much they want to settle

your case. If it's a decent amount we'll accept it with the mediator's help, but if the offer is ridiculous we'll demand the jury. Let me talk to their insurance attorneys first. We already set up a meeting just to discuss where we stand after all the depositions. Let's see what they offer us then I'll get back to you."

Three months passed, and Marsha had no contact with her attorney. Finally, she called to inquire what happened in the interim. When she hung up the phone she realized to her greatest shock that Mr. Monty no longer called her by her first name but very formally kept addressing her as Dr. Redcliff. He ended the phone call abruptly with "I did not get all the information, yet, and will get back to you later."

Marsha placed several phone calls and left messages with the law firm's secretary before Mr. Monty contacted her after another five or six weeks later. He claimed the negotiations with the attorneys representing the malpractice insurance companies went very poorly. He got an offer of less than one-thousand dollars in total reimbursement of every wrong-doing and subsequent damage. The one-thousand dollars were to be rewarded for the missed diagnosis of cancer, for the undiagnosed and not treated infection, losing her right lung, losing her work, all her suffering and losses. On the other hand he emphasized that the opposition team was very sympathetic to her case. The legal representation of both malpractice attorneys were sad about her situation and highly complementary to her and her lawyer.

"Of course the offer is neither realistic nor acceptable so I recommend you to wait until after the five year anniversary of your surgery. *With a little luck the cancer would recur by then.* In that case we would have a real strong law suit."

"Did you hear what you just said?" Marsha could

not decide whether her shock or her insult was worse. "In order that you possibly get a better outcome of my claim, you just wished the recurrence of the lung cancer on me."

"Well, you shouldn't interpret it that way. You have to realize you don't have a solid case against them. You need more supportive evidence, that's all."

"This is not how you talked to me before," the bewildered Marsha snapped, "You promised me a jury, and judge, and a 'big gun' you would use. Do you remember all those promises? Don't tell me that suddenly you discovered I have no case at all. What happened to your conviction, how come you lost it? What happened in your meeting with the insurance reps that convinced you otherwise? Your change occurred just as soon as you met the lawyers. I am sure the timing was purely coincidental."

"You do have a case; it's just not worth anything. No question, the negligence was proven. But no financial losses occurred or minimal, at best. The law is based upon the monetary deficit resulting from the negligence. And don't even start on the personal suffering because I cannot put a pecuniary figure on that." The lawyer conveniently ignored Marsha's last question.

"A what? What is a pecuniary figure?"

"It means monetary figures. Money to be awarded." Mr. Monty's voice took on a cold tone.

"Ok, thanks. So this is how this plays out. The offer essentially means no punishment for them and an outright insult for me. In the interim, both Ramsey and Katsui continue to criminally neglect and injure others. Terrific! What else can be done? Is there anything else? Please understand me. I don't want these two clowns to get away with murder and continue the same practice day in and day out, just because they had a better legal representative than me. I don't care about the money. I have enough, more than what I need. I just want to stop them."

"Then you should have contacted the Medical Board and not an attorney. You should have written them a letter and file a complaint." Mr. Monty replied with ease.

"Why haven't you advised me of this option before now? I never heard you ever mention it in any of our meetings. Would you write a letter now to the Board?"

Marsha thought, she did not hear his answer well. "No, this is your job. We have invested enough. We cannot do more. Our law firm is a one attorney operation. We cannot afford to spend more time on this case. One does not invest more money in such circumstances." The distinguished-looking Mr. Monty smoothly elevated to a higher level of moral indignity and ended the clearly futile discussion. He washed his hands like Pontius Pilate and from then on, he was too busy to return her phone calls.

After she became aware of the abrupt and drastic change, Marsha mentally reviewed her dialogues with Mr. Monty. She always thought only love, power, and money could motivate a man enough to transform his conviction and love was out of the equation in this situation. She wondered if perhaps the three other lawyers she met during her deposition and who represented the insurance companies, offered Mr. Monty opportunities to work with them in future malpractice cases. They also must have praised and complimented him, after all, fork tongues often drip with honey.

They could have intimidated him with their mega-dollar corporate back-up or they projected the case would drag out without a foreseeable end and becoming a true money-pit for a solo legal practice. It seemed logical, because Mr. Monty's drastic change occurred exactly the week after all attorneys had the conference. Of course, she kept her suspicion wordless and voiceless. She could never prove her inkling. Lawyers had the ability to rise above the moral level of common folks and in their indignation over claimed insults, quickly sued for defamation of a character.

What was she to do? Would another attorney take up her botched up case? Was there an attorney in the entire state who would sue a teammate just to take up her crusade? Do sharks bite other sharks? Do vultures dig out the eyes of other vultures? Even if she could find one, the new counselor would have to reimburse Mr. Monty's expenses first. What would the new lawyer get? Not enough to invest time and energy in a lost cause.

Her suspicion was confirmed by the prestigious Schwartz, Meyven, and Lebowitz Manhattan Law firm. They reviewed her claim and agreed with her but did not take the case. In their opinion the new attorney would have to repeat all the botched up depositions of the insufficiently interrogated physicians. As of now, the failure pointed at Marsha, herself, for being non-compliant according to Dr. Ramsey's unchallenged, sworn testimony. The duplication of preliminary work would add a significant sum to the expenses. It was not promising enough money to pay both Mr. Monty and their firm. Sorry Dr. Redcliff, yours was the moral victory only.

Marsha sent a letter to the State Board of Medicine and supported her statement with copies of her medical records and chest CT. The response for the HIPAA violation of Dr. Ramsey's indiscretion merited nothing but a categorical denial. No reasons given, just kicked out to the curb.

"So much for the constantly emphasized protection of privacy," murmured Marsha. Once the rules were broken by someone, apparently there were no consequences put in place for remediation. The constantly hyped up protection was only a lot of malarkey, pure hot air. Nothing more.

From the Board of Medicine a man contacted her in response to her complaints. He was well-versed in her documents, he seemed sympathetic, and asked several poignant questions. At the end he gave her his direct phone number and advised her that he would forward the paper trail with his findings to the next higher echelon, the Office of the General Counsel's Prosecution Services Unit. Marsha cautiously started to hope again.

Seven months later, Marsha received an official letter stating the Florida Department of Health (DOH) closed its investigation and dismissed her claim for "lack of finding of probable cause". Indeed, doctors acted as sharks and vultures: neither harmed the other. The Office of the General Counsel silently dismissed the complaint against Dr. Ramsey and Dr. Katsui thus protecting the guilty and allowing to propagate the same conduct in a neglectful practice. The bushel of apples slowly and surely rotted from the decaying apple hiding within. The DOH's job was to safeguard the health of the citizens; yet, by ignoring a grave complaint, they absolutely failed this task. The lack of action and silence deafeningly announced their bias. The Department of Health ruled, and according to their judgement Marsha's letter of complaint was not worthy to generate a simple letter of warning to either physicians.

Sorry, Dr. Redcliff, yours was the moral victory only.

30

*Never insult an alligator until after
you have crossed the river.*

———

Cordell Hull

Cecilia Beach Hospital was busy with the flu season. When all beds were occupied, the waiting rooms were converted to makeshift hospital rooms. Every physician and nurse worked overtime and an added bonus was offered for taking extra shifts.

In the very midst of the epidemic Dr. Pribus broke his ankle. He was on call and was rushing to get his charging cell phone from another room when he slipped and fell. His left leg slid ahead of him and as he fell backward, he landed on his bent right leg with his full body weight. He heard three distinct cracking sounds, one after the other, before he temporarily lost consciousness. A few minutes later and still in a daze, he looked at his fast swollen ankle to realize the damage was great. Although the ankle was deformed, he hoped it was only due to a dislocation and not a fracture. When he finally managed to pull himself up from the floor, he learned it otherwise. His right foot freely swung and the pain almost pushed him to lose his mind. He realized he needed help and quick.

In the ER Dr. Ferguson immediately medicated him

for the pain and then told him the X-ray confirmed compound fractures and dislocation. He admitted his colleague for surgery but first under sedation he repositioned the broken bones of the ankle joint.

Dr. Taylor was the orthopedic surgeon on call. After looking at the X-ray films, he decided the surgery was beyond his expertise. He called for consultation by the University Hospital's orthopedic surgeon. Unfortunately, he was advised the surgeon was away and not expected to return until the end of the following week. His colleague just left for a conference across the country. The only available orthopedic specialist was a hand surgeon. Next, Dr. Taylor called Administration, but Mr. Lawler firmly advised him to follow the unwritten rules and buy time until their own orthopedic surgeon was available.

Pribus was in immense agony. The slightest movement of his right leg sent white hot poker pain all the way to his brain and although being a doctor and a man, he repeatedly begged for pain medication. When Dr. Taylor finally confronted him with the fact that his surgery was put on hold, he forcefully concentrated enough to get out of his foggy medicated existence and demanded to be transferred anywhere to get the surgery done. Dr. Taylor did not know where to send him but promised to investigate the possibilities and return with some suggestions. Pribus never laid eyes on him again.

On the third day Mr. Lawler visited the unfortunate hospitalist. Sitting by Dr. Pribus' bedside, he cheerfully chatted about every hospital-related business and then assured him, "You are part of the family and we will take good care of you. If you need anything, just pick up the phone and call me. I am here for you, I hope you know that. Is there anything I can do before I leave?"

"If you could find out when my surgery is ... I would be grateful. This is the third day and no one seems to know," he winced as the pain medication was wearing off and his leg started to throb again.

"The way I understood from Dr. Taylor you have a complicated fracture and no available surgeon can do the repair now. When the doctor from UH comes back from his vacation, we'll transfer you there. We have a contract with them, so it's like being within our own system. But don't worry, in the interim we'll transfer you to a nursing home and when the surgery is scheduled, we'll get you back. How does that sound to you? OK?" Mr. Lawler smiled.

"No, it's not OK. This is an acute fracture. It needs to be repaired. Actually, it was supposed to be an emergency surgery. Frankly, I don't care who does the surgery; that is, I don't care if he or she is from within our system or not. My insurance covers all providers, not only the Cecilia Beach Hospitals. I should be transferred immediately to someone who can operate on my leg."

"I know, I know, but wouldn't you rather remain within our family? I am sure you would be better off with your colleagues taking care of you, don't you think? I guarantee you to have your surgery the very next day the orthopedic surgeon returns from his vacation. Come now, it's not such a long wait, either, it's less than two weeks. In the meantime, we would take good care of you. As the CEO of this hospital I can tell you we certainly would prefer it this way," Mr. Lawler pushed his agenda while placing extra weight on his authority.

"If it cannot be done here and now, then transfer me to the Cleveland Clinic in Weston or the Mayo Clinic in Jacksonville. Either one should have plenty of capable surgeons to do the work before gangrene sets into the splintered bones." Pribus called the nurse to reposition his leg and repeat his pain medication. During the commotion, Mr. Lawler slipped away without being noticed.

Pribus asked his colleagues for recommendations. He soon learned that one of the best ankle and foot specialist of the entire state recently moved to less than ten miles from the hospital but he was affiliated with another health care system.

The bewildered and horrified hospitalist realized Mr. Lawler refused him to be transferred to this specialist; instead he wanted to wait for his own surgeon to return from vacation. The pain and suffering of the broken bones or the increasing risk of complications didn't matter. The almighty dollar was the only motivator.

Dr. Pribus called the specialty surgeon but the man apologized as he was ready to leave the next morning, "If I did the operation there was no one to follow up with the post-operative care. You understand, I cannot abandon a patient once I get involved. I wish they had called me when it happened; by now you would be ready to go to rehab. Sorry."

Later on in the day Josè stopped by and wondered why no one called Dr. Valdon. True, he was not one of the hospital-owned doctors but he rented an office in the adjoining Medical Arts Building and was privileged in the hospital.

"All they want is the money; trust me, that's the problem. Dr. Valdon is good, but he is an independent orthopedic surgeon. He also has his own X-ray, and his own physical therapy and rehabilitation people, and does not use the hospital's. I guess Mr. Lawler does not want to lose all that money to an outsider so they make you wait." Realizing what he said, Josè quickly added, "Please keep the info I gave you between us and don't quote me, because I would have to deny I ever said it."

Pribus could not move. His right leg was propped up on two pillows but no one ever gave him an ice pack, they just pushed the injectable analgesic and alternated it with the pain pills. He never took anything stronger than either a Tylenol or Motrin before and was not used to the strong drugs he needed now. The fourth afternoon he woke up to much yelling and tugging at him. He vaguely noted some familiar faces around him but he could not comprehend why they yelled at him, "Say 'school', spell it! Spell the word 'school'."

He thought it was funny but he said it 'scuola' and spelled it s-c-u-o-l-a.

"No, spell 'school'. The word school. Do you hear me? Or say 'hospital'. Can you spell it?" The charge nurse instructed him.

"Of course, 'ospitale', o-s-p-i-t-a-l-e." Pribus concentrated and thought he said it clearly so why were the nurses standing all around him, insisting on him saying it again? Once more, quite deliberately, he spelled both words and was satisfied with his own response.

Then he unmistakably heard the charge nurse say "Give him a dose of Narcan, I will get the order from his attending later." Narcan? The medication Narcan was to reverse the opioid caused over-sedation. Pribus wondered why he needed it, but he had difficulty to concentrate and his eyes felt too heavy to open. Oh well, let them do whatever they want to as long as they let him sleep. After the medication took effect and he was more alert, they laughingly told him, "You were talking gibberish and needed the Narcan, big time."

Pribus quietly told them, "No, I was not. I remember you asked me to spell the word 'school' and I spelled it correctly. Then you asked me to do the same for 'hospital' and I repeatedly said it. It was not gibberish. It was Italian.

I reverted to my native language, that's all. Any of you guys speak Italian?" Dr. Pribus looked from nurse to nurse but each shook her head.

"Ok guys, I will teach you something. We all learn other languages throughout our lives. Let's say your native language is English. But at age ten you move to Spain so you learn Spanish. Then you go to a university in Paris so you have to speak French, too. But if you marry a German man by chance then you probably learn to speak German as well. Skip several decades all the way until you get old and get diagnosed with Alzheimer's disease, and something interesting happens. You would eventually forget all the languages you learned, but you forget them in reverse order. So first you lose German then gradually fail at French, and finally you cannot recall any Spanish words. If you're still alive, you may get sparser and sparser vocabulary in English but the native language is what you preserve the longest. Your mother's tongue, the early learned first language remains with you the longest. The same thing happens with the anesthesia drugs and pain medicine: you gave me too much and I reverted to my native Italian. That's all."

"It sounded gibberish," the charge nurse defended herself.

"Well, I'll tell you what, from now on, I will put on my resume that I speak English, Italian and Gibberish. How is that?" Diplomatic Dr. Pribus solved the dilemma. They all laughed and peace returned to the nurses' station immediately.

On the fifth day after the accident Dr. Valdon repaired the broken bones by placing three screws, eight pins, and a seven-inch long plate in his right leg. In two more days he was transferred to a rehabilitation center and then returned to Dr. Valdon's therapy for more exercises.

After Dr. Pribus recovered, he referred to his ankle repair as half of Home Depot's hardware was put in his leg to make it work again.

He did not give a second thought about Mr. Lawler's and Cecilia Beach Hospital system's financial losses at all.

31

Life, if well lived, is long enough.

———

Lucius Annaeus Seneca

The phone rang in the Redcliff residence. Marsha was surprised because her work phone was silent since her surgery. True, it was three months ago when she underwent the operation but she was still recovering. The hospital gave her a leave of absence expecting her to come back as soon as she was able to carry out her duties as a neurologist.

"Dr. Redcliff. May I help you?" The old routine answer returned, seemingly almost uninterrupted.

"Sorry to bother you Dr. Redcliff, but I have to relay a message to you."

"What's going on Josè? I recognized your voice at the first moment you started to talk. 'Long time no hear' as the Chinese would say."

"Dr. Bell is in the ICU. We think he had a stroke. He asked for you. Do you think you could come by to see him? Are you up to it?"

"Of course, I will see him. He is not only a colleague, but a very fine doctor, too. He has always been my friend. Sure, I will go," Marsha did not hesitate for a second.

"The problem is, it's not only a visit he needs. He does not want any other neurologist but you. He said you would help him if you knew he was ill. Do you think you could?" Josè asked.

"I hope so Josè. It may take me a little time but please assure him I will be there today."

"I knew you would Dr. Redcliff. I could always count on you. Thank you! Take it easy and look for me if you need any help when you arrive. I will be at the front desk. See you later and thanks again." Josè hung up the phone.

It was late afternoon by the time Marsha got herself together and drove to the hospital. The return felt like a homecoming: nothing changed since her last visit and she felt comfortable and confident once more. As soon as she sat by the computer to read Dr. Bell's medical history, all of the sudden her anxiety dissipated and gave room to objective thinking, knowledge, and cool self-assurance.

She already forgot the careful way she had to dress while gingerly avoiding movements which pulled the freshly healed scar. She overlooked the initial discomfort she had as she slid onto the car seat and started to drive. It was over three months ago when she worked the last time and now her anxiety was overwhelming. How long these three months seemed now! Practically every week there were new medications and new tests available. How many would she encounter after being away for these long months? She was getting anxious just thinking of the challenges awaiting her.

All along the drive she talked to herself about her new neurological case.

> I hope it was a simple stroke and they did
> the correct steps of treatment as soon as he
> had the first symptoms.

Oh, and I expect they ordered the right work up, not just a simple CT scan. I better check the ultrasound and MRI images before I see him.

Poor Dr. Bell, he should be on preventive medications by now. I have to see whether he got the correct dose of each.

Wow, I did not think he was old enough to have a stroke. But then he might have had some obscure reason to get it. I have to find the underlying cause to treat him and prevent a recurrence effectively.

Maybe he had a heart disease, an irregular beat which sent a blood clot to his brain. Or he had a clot within the chamber of the heart. I better get an echocardiogram and an MRA picture of his brain and neck vessels, if any seemed to have an abrupt cut-off then I know where the problem was.

Don't forget to call Dr. Anderson to evaluate his heart, I have to remember that. In the interim, I should get an echocardiogram.

He seemed to be too healthy and if no obvious cause for a stroke, maybe he had a blood disorder and clotted abnormally. Or perhaps an obscure malignancy. I must keep this in my mind, too, and investigate it.

She started to pray. Nothing traditional, not reciting any childhood formal prayer embedded in her mind for decades. She rather talked to God as if she were sitting next to him and she could sound out her concerns and ask for his help.

Lord, help me so I avoid missing the correct diagnosis.

Don't let me make the wrong assumption or use improper treatments.

Give me the strength of the body to withhold physical distress.

Grant me the knowledge, let all the things I ever heard and learned in medicine be ready in my mind to be retrieved instantly to benefit my patient.

Disquiet my anxiety and strengthen my self-confidence.

Share with me your love to humankind so I could love the poor suffering man the same way.

Let my kindness and empathy shine through my actions to give comfort and a sense of security to those I attend.

I remember what the old preacher Mr. Tanner thought me: say to each patient, "When I touch you, I touch the face of God." Let me be as good as he was. Let me see your face in each suffering human.

And above all Lord, guide me in my work by your right hand --- but please keep your left over my mouth in the interim.

As she entered through the ICU doors she was once again the composed, self-confident neurologist, radiating calmness and kindness.

As soon as she read Dr. Bell's history, a stroke diagnosis made no sense. He had fluctuating symptoms over the last couple of months. It started with a weird sensation of lightheadedness, almost as if he were transiently weightless and floating. Dr. Bell ignored it, blaming the cause to be his long hours of work and uncomfortable pillow. Then he developed frank dizziness, almost to the level of losing consciousness. That scared him enough to seek a medical evaluation. All his laboratory results were within normal range and nothing pinpointed to a serious underlying disorder. The dizzy spells continued until he was found unconscious on the floor behind his desk and was brought to the ER.

Physically he was in great shape, without any deficits. The CT scan was negative but it didn't mean much to Marsha. She knew the back of the brain was poorly represented by a CT because of the reflection of the curved bones of the occiput often masked soft tissue disease, especially in the case of a small lesion. The hospitalist thought it was a psychosomatic disorder. After all, as a physician Dr. Bell knew too much, as a man he was probably overexcited by his symptoms, and as a person he might have harbored a trifle of hypochondriac disorder. Regardless, he was treated with kind deference, as one treats a mentally unstable man.

Marsha stared at the MR images for a long time. She had an uneasy feeling and the longer she studied the brainstem area the stronger the ill feeling became. She was sure Dr. Bell didn't experience a stroke. It was something by far worse, something which she would have to tell him and she did not know how to do it. An indistinct shadow encroached the brainstem and indented it. The lesion was surrounded by a minimal but unmistakable edema further pressing on the brainstem. Dr. Bell had an invasive malignancy at the worst possible location. It was fatal.

What can I offer him? There was no surgery to save him. By the time the surgeon would reach the area, he might die from the damage done on the way in alone. I could get him to an oncologist but he would know it just as well as I do that all measures would be only holy water sprinkled on him occasionally and very sparingly. Dr. Bell was doomed. It was only a matter of time and probably not a long time, either, judging by his escalating symptoms.

Lord, I asked for your help. Now I really need it. Guide me to find the right words when I talk to him. Let me strengthen his hope while gently leading him to accept the inevitable. Let me be his hope. Let me be his strength. Let me help him.

She entered his room with a wide smile and warmly shook his hand, "My dear Dr. Bell, you certainly could have called me for a friendly visit instead of getting me here as your neurologist. My, my, some men would do anything to get me! Hmm, I always wanted to see you in your pajamas but never imagined it would be in the ICU. Is this the only way you could manage to be the center of attraction?" She noted Dr. Bell's facial expression gradually lost tension and he became relaxed and smiled as he kept pumping her hand.

"Seriously, I was honored by your friendship before and now it would be my privilege to assist you. Tell me what happened," Marsha sat down by the bedside of her colleague.

An hour later Dr. Bell asked Marsha if he could be referred to a good oncologist. She recommended him to the Moffitt Center. Before she said good night to Dr. Bell, he shyly asked her to come closer so he could kiss her hand.

"My, don't make me feel like a holy relic! Give me a hug and we'll see each other tomorrow. You have a date with me here, don't you forget and don't go anywhere! You better remember you are my captive audience," Marsha joked.

On the way home she was stopped by a policeman.

Instead of getting a ticket, the man recognized her and joyfully recalled how Marsha explained to him that his distorted face was not caused by a devastating stroke but it was the result of a simple Bell's palsy. He quickly recited the stroke symptoms and risk factors, exactly the way she taught him. Afterward he added, "I taught everyone at the precinct the same way you taught me. Imagine, I became the expert, thanks to you," he boasted.

After a year he still felt the gratitude and he let her go, "You were the only nice person in the ER because you listened to me when nobody else would. I was only just another disease to them, but to you I was a human being. A sick and scared human being. In return, I want to be nice to you, too. Your rear light is out on the right. Get it fixed as soon as you get home."

Looking at the beaming face of the policeman, it occurred to Marsha that maybe she touched more people and added more to life than she ever knew. Perhaps she should not doubt herself but give herself credit for her contributions. It dawned on her that she could not disappear; she would not completely dissolve when the end claimed her. The physical presence would be replaced by the memories attached to her and her ideas and sayings. Her work would be carried on by others.

The world will not change, the Earth will spin the same way as before, and Cecilia Beach Hospital will be run exactly the same as when she worked there. But as long as someone like this policeman would remember her, she would live on. She was convinced beyond a shadow of doubt that many parts of her would survive the old shell called a "body". Her actions, her kindness, her teachings, her care would continue to exist and immortalize her.

Suddenly her heart became full and overflowed. She became conscious of being an irreplaceable part of the universe. For the first time in her life, she comprehended her unique role in it and claimed ownership over the part. Without forming any words or thoughts, she accepted and appreciated all things around her. She was content with her life: she made her mark.

Life was good and it was worth living.

ABOUT THE AUTHOR

Angela Sréter Spencer was born in Transylvania, raised in Hungary but lived most of her adult life in the US. She showed early interest in literature, following in the footsteps of her ancestors.

She has always had a steadfast optimism and unwavering faith in the goodness and godliness of mankind. This conviction enabled her to overcome all obstacles and helped to retain her belief of eternal permanence in the ever changing picture of life. It also helped her to successfully transform to become a cerebrovascular neurologist in her late fifties. She resides in Florida, and is currently certified by the American Board of Psychiatry and Neurology.

Two Candles (2010) was her first published book of poems, beautifully illustrated by László Hopp's award winning photographic art. Her poetry is listed in the prestigious "International Who Is Who in Poetry".

Dating Games (2012) is a collection of short stories, originating from the many interviews she conducted both in private and professional setting.

Land of Cotton (2015) is a psychological suspense-murder novel, guaranteed the reader guessing who the ultimate criminal could be.

Community Hospital (2020) is her latest work, dedicated to patients and health care professionals, recommending the need of a reliable and educated advocate to assist at all times to help and navigate through the dangerous areas of medical diagnosis and treatment.